There can
gorgeous n
off in front

Even as she tol
the scene in front of her was a figment of her
imagination, Emily watched him kick off his boots,
then with one smooth jerk, toss his pants aside.
She was spellbound. Vaguely, she heard the crowd
yelling, urging him on. He looked away from her
finally, releasing her from his dark gaze. But still
she watched him.

He was the most beautiful man she'd ever seen.
Raw, sexual, but also...gentle. Her heart raced as
the officer...obviously *not* an officer, started
toward her. His eyes, a pale, fierce green, reflected
the spotlight. He stared directly at her, then moved
so close she could smell the clean male fragrance
of him, could feel his body heat. And God, was he
hot!

Panting, unable to stop herself, Emily realized he
was waiting for her to give him money. Of all the
insane ideas...but there were numerous bills
sticking out of those small briefs, and she knew he
wouldn't budge until she'd done as he silently
commanded.

She fumbled in her pockets, then stuck out her
hand, offering him her money. He smiled wickedly,
then with a small, barely discernible motion, he
shook his head, nodding downward.

Her eyes locked on his cash-filled briefs—and
what they were hiding....

Dear Reader,

Starting this month, Temptation turns up the *heat*. We'd like to introduce you to our newest miniseries— bold, provocative, *ultrasexy* books that could only be called BLAZE. Throughout the year be sure to watch for these red-hot reads from Temptation.

#629 OUTRAGEOUS—
Lori Foster (April 1997)

#639 RESTLESS NIGHTS—
Tiffany White (June 1997)

#648 OUT OF CONTROL—
Candace Schuler (August 1997)

#649 NIGHT RHYTHMS—
Elda Minger (Sept. 1997)

We hope these exciting new stories will compel you to experience the heroines' euphoria of achieving their fantasies—and inspire you to fulfill a few fantasies of your own.

Happy Reading,

The Editors

It's hot...and it's out of control!

OUTRAGEOUS
Lori Foster

Harlequin Books

TORONTO • NEW YORK • LONDON
AMSTERDAM • PARIS • SYDNEY • HAMBURG
STOCKHOLM • ATHENS • TOKYO • MILAN
MADRID • WARSAW • BUDAPEST • AUCKLAND

To Dianne Kruetzkamp,
A very special friend who's fond of saying,
"This is the best one yet."
I'll never tire of hearing it. Thanks.

And to Stella Cameron,
Your insight, advice and friendship are priceless,
just like your stories.
The industry is lucky to have you, and so am I.

ISBN 0-373-25729-5

OUTRAGEOUS

Copyright © 1997 by Lori Foster.

This edition published by arrangement with Harlequin Books S.A.

® and TM are trademarks of the publisher. Trademarks indicated with
® are registered in the United States Patent and Trademark Office, the
Canadian Trade Marks Office and in other countries.

Printed in U.S.A.

1

SHE HAD the biggest brown eyes Judd had ever seen.

She also looked innocent as hell, despite the ridiculous clothes she wore and the huge, frayed canvas tote bag she carried. Did she actually think she blended in, just because her coat was tattered and her hat was a little ratty? Did she think anyone would ever believe her to be homeless? Not likely.

So what was she doing here at this time of night? The lower east side of Springfield was no place for a lady like her. She strolled past him again, this time more slowly, and her eyes were so wide it looked as if they could take in her surroundings in a single glance. They took in Judd.

He felt a thrill of awareness, sharper than anything he'd ever felt before. She looked away, but not before he detected the faint pink blush that washed over her fine features. That blush had been obvious even in the dim evening light, with only the moon and corner street lamp for illumination. She had flawless skin.

Dammit. He had enough to worry about without some damn Miss Priss with manicured nails and salon-styled hair trying to fob herself off as a local. Judd had only stepped outside the bar to get a breath of fresh air.

The smell of perfume inside was overwhelming, and enough to turn his stomach.

He could hear the music in the bar grow louder and knew the dancers were coming onstage. In less than ten minutes, he'd have to go back in there, baring himself in the line of duty.

Damn. He hated this cover. What decent, hardworking cop should have to peel off his clothes for a bunch of sex-starved, groping women? For nearly two weeks now he'd been entertaining the female masses with the sight of his body, hoping to uncover enough evidence to make a bust. He was now, at thirty-two, in his prime, more fit than ever and completely alone. Not only did he meet the necessary requirements to pull off such a ludicrous cover, he had a vested, very personal interest this time. He knew for a fact the room above the bar was the site for shady business meetings, yet he hadn't seen hide nor hair of a gun deal. Clayton Donner was laying low.

It was discouraging, but he wasn't giving up.

He was definitely going to get Donner, but that didn't mean he enjoyed displaying himself nightly.

Each of the strippers had a gimmick. He thought his was rather ironic. He played out the tough street cop, complete with black pants held together with strategically placed Velcro. They came off with only the smallest tug. He even had Max's original leather jacket—a prized possession, to be sure—to add to his authenticity. The women loved it.

He wondered if old Max had known how sexy the cop persona was to females. Or if he would have cared.

God, he couldn't think about Max and still do his job, which was to appear unscrupulous enough that Donner would think him available. Clayton always needed new pigeons to run his scams. Judd intended to be the next. It was the only way he could get close enough to make a clean bust.

And the last thing he needed now was a distraction with big brown eyes. Despite his resolve, his gaze wandered back to the woman. She was loitering on the corner beneath the street lamp, holding that large, lumpy bag to her chest and trying to fit in. Judd snorted. That old coat was buttoned so high she was damn near strangling herself. What the hell was she doing here?

He'd just about convinced himself not to care, not to get involved, when three young men seemed to notice her. Judd watched as they approached her. She started to back away, then evidently changed her mind. She nodded a greeting, but it was a wimpy effort. Hell, the men looked determined to get to know her, without any encouragement on her part. She, on the other hand, looked ready to faint.

Walk away, he thought, willing the woman to move. But she stood her ground. He sensed, then he knew for certain, she was getting in over her head. His body was already tensing, his eyes narrowed, waiting for the trouble to start. They seemed to be talking, or, more to the point, she was trying to speak to them. She gestured with her hands, her expression earnest. Then one of the men grabbed her and she let loose a startled screech. In the next instant, those huge brown eyes of hers turned his way, demanding that he help her.

The little twit thought he was a regular street cop. At this rate she'd blow his cover.

Well, hell, he couldn't allow her to be manhandled. He pushed himself away from the doorway and started forward. The men were obviously drunk. One of them was doing his best to pull her close, but she kept side-stepping him. Judd approached them all with a casual air.

"Here now, boys." He kept his tone low and deep, deliberately commanding. "Why don't you leave the lady alone."

Judd could see her trembling, could see the paleness of her face in the yellow light of the street lamp. The man didn't release her; if anything, he tightened his grip. "Go to hell."

The words were slurred, and Judd wondered just how drunk they were. They might believe him to be a cop, but in this neighborhood, being a law enforcement officer carried very little clout and regularly drew vicious disdain. Damn.

He couldn't get into a brawl—he might literally lose his pants. Not that he wouldn't enjoy knocking some heads together, but still.... Where was a real uniformed cop when you needed one?

He turned his gaze on the woman. "Do you want their company?"

She swallowed, her throat working convulsively. "No."

One of the men shook his fist in Judd's face, stumbling drunkenly as he did so. "She's already made a deal with us." The man grinned stupidly at the woman, then added, "You can't expect a little thing like her to run around here without a weapon to protect herself..."

One of the other men slugged the speaker. "Shut up, you fool."

Judd went very still, scrutinizing the woman's face. "Well?"

Again, she swallowed. "Well...what?"

"Why do you need a weapon? You planning to kill someone?" Whisper-soft, his question still demanded an immediate answer.

Shaking her head, then looking around as if desperately seeking a means of escape, she managed to pique his interest. He couldn't walk away now. Whatever she was up to, she didn't want him to know. Because she thought he was a cop?

Disgusted, Judd propped his hands on his hips, his eyebrows drawn together in a frown. "Do you want the company of these men or not?"

She peered cautiously at the drunken, leering face so close to her own. Her lips tightened in disapproval and disdain. "Ah...no. Not particularly."

A genuine smile tipped his mouth before he caught himself. She had gumption, he'd give her that. She was no bigger than a ten-year-old sickly kid. The coat she wore practically swallowed her up. She was fine-boned, petite, and everything about her seemed fragile. "There you go, fellas. The lady doesn't find you to her liking. Turn her loose and go find something else to do."

"I got somethin' to do already." Her captor's hold seemed to loosen just a bit as he spoke, and taking advantage, she suddenly jerked free. Then she did the dumbest thing Judd had ever seen. She sent her knee into the man's groin.

Unbelievable. Judd shook his head, even as he yanked her behind him, trying to protect her from the ensuing chaos. He couldn't do any real damage to the men without attracting more spectators, which would threaten his cover. And the woman was gasping behind him, scared out of her wits from the sound of it. But damn it all, he definitely *did not* want to lose his pants out here scuffling in the middle of the sidewalk with common drunks. One of the men started to throw a punch.

Judd cursed loudly as the woman ran around him, evidently not as frightened as he'd thought, and leaped onto his attacker's back. She couldn't weigh over a hundred pounds, but she wound her fingers in the man's hair and pulled with all her might.

Enough was enough. A glimpse at his watch told him it was time for his performance. Judd grabbed the man away from her and sent him reeling with a firm kick to the rear end, then stalked the other two, every muscle in his body tensed. Too drunk to persist in their efforts, the men scurried away.

Judd turned to face the woman, and she was...

tidying her hair? Good God, was she nuts? He saw her look toward her canvas bag, which now lay in a puddle on the sidewalk, but she made no move to retrieve it.

"You don't want your bag?" he asked with all the sarcasm he could muster.

"Oh." She glanced at him. "Well, of course..." She made a move in its direction, but he shook his head. He could see more raggedy clothing falling out the opening, and if there was one thing this woman didn't need, it was hand-me-downs.

He took her arm in a firm but gentle hold, ignoring her resistance, and started her toward the bar. He automatically moved her to his right side, bringing her between his body and the building, protecting her from passersby. He held his temper for all of about three seconds, then gave up the effort.

"Of all the stupid, *harebrained*...lady, what the hell did you think you were doing back there?" He wondered if she could be a journalist, or a TV newswoman? She damn well wasn't used to living in alleys, or going without. Everything about her screamed money. Even now, with him hustling her down the sidewalk, she had a certain grace, a definite poise, that didn't come from being underprivileged.

She glanced up at him, and he noticed she smelled nice, too. Not heavily perfumed like the women in the bar, just...very feminine. Her wavy shoulder-length hair, a light brown that looked as baby soft as her eyes, bounced as he hurried her along. She was practically running, but he couldn't help that. He was going to be late. He could hear the music for his number starting. Taking off his clothes in public was bad enough. He didn't intend to make a grand entrance by jumping in late.

She cleared her throat. "I appreciate your assistance, Officer."

Without slowing his pace, he glared at her. "Answer my question. Who are you? What the hell are you up to?"

"That's two questions."

He growled, his patience at an end. "*Answer me, dammit!*"

She stumbled, then glared up at him defiantly. "That's really none of your business."

Everything inside his body clenched. "I'm making it my business."

Digging in her heels as he tried to haul her through the front door, she forced him to slow down. She was wide-eyed again and he noticed her mouth was hanging open as he dragged her into the bar. "What are you doing?"

There was a note of shrill panic in her voice as she took in her surroundings. Judd had no time to explain, and no time to consider her delicate sensibilities. Everyone in this part of town thought of him as a money-hungry, oversexed, willing exhibitionist—Clayton Donner included. It was a necessary cover and one he wasn't ready to forfeit. Donner would show up again soon, and once he decided Judd was a familiar face in the area, the gun dealer would make his move. It would happen. He'd make it happen.

Still gripping her arm, Judd trotted her toward the nearest bar stool. *"Stay right here."* He stared down at her, trying to intimidate her with his blackest scowl. The music was picking up tempo, signaling his cue.

She popped right back off the seat, those eyes of hers accurately portraying her shock. "Now see here! I have no intention of waiting—"

He picked her up, dropped her onto the stool again, then called to the bartender. "Keep her here, Freddie. Make certain she doesn't budge."

Freddie, a huge, jovial sort with two front teeth missing, grinned and nodded. "What'd she do?"

"She owes me. Big. Keep your eye on her."

"And if she tries to pike it?"

Judd gave Freddie a conspiratorial wink. "Make her sorry if she so much as flinches."

Freddie looked ferocious, but Judd knew he wouldn't hurt a fly. That was the reason they had not one, but two bouncers on the premises. But the little lady didn't know that, and Judd wanted to find out exactly what she was up to. Gut instinct told him he wouldn't like what he found.

Suddenly the spotlight swirled around the floor. Cursing, then forcing a grin to his mouth, Judd sauntered forward into the light. Women screamed.

In the short time he'd been performing here, he'd discovered a wealth of information about his gun dealer...and become a favorite of the bar. The owner had promised to double his pay, but that was nothing compared to the bills that always ended up stuffed in his skimpy briefs. He refused, absolutely *refused*, to wear a G-string. His naked butt was not something he showed to more than one woman at a time, and even *those* exhibitions were few and far between. But his modesty worked to his advantage. The women customers thought he was a tease, and appreciated his show all the more.

As he moved, he glanced over his shoulder to make certain the lady was still there. She hadn't moved. She didn't look as though she could. Her eyes were even larger now, huge and luminous and filled with shock and disbelief. He held her gaze, and slowly, backing into the center of the floor, slid the zipper down on the leather jacket. He saw her gasp.

Her intent expression, of innocence mixed with curious wonder, annoyed him, making him feel more exposed than he ever had while performing. That he could feel his face heat angered him. He was too old, and too cynical now, to actually blush. *Damn her.*

Purposefully holding her gaze, determined to make her look away, he let his fingers move to the top of his pants. As he slowly unhooked the fly, one snap at a time, teasing his audience, teasing her more, she reeled back and one dainty hand touched her chest. She looked distressed. She looked shocked.

But she didn't look away.

OH, LORD. Oh, Lord. This can't be happening, Emily! It's too outrageous. There can't possibly be a large, gorgeous man peeling his clothes off in front of you.

Even as she told herself she was delirious, that the scene in front of her was a figment of her fantastical imagination, Emily watched him kick off his boots, then with one smooth jerk, toss his pants aside. She wouldn't have missed a single instant of his disrobing. She couldn't. She was spellbound.

Vaguely, in the back of her mind, she heard the crowd yelling, urging him on. He looked away from her finally, releasing her from his dark gaze. But still she watched him.

He was the most beautiful man she'd ever seen. Raw, sexual, but also...gentle. She could feel his gentleness, had felt it outside when she'd first walked past him. It was as if she recognized he didn't belong here, in this seedy neighborhood, any more than she did.

But they *were* both here. Her reason was plain; she needed to find out who had sold her younger brother the gun that backfired, nearly causing him to lose an eye. He would recover, but that wouldn't remove the fact that he'd bought the gun illegally, that he was involved in something he had no business being involved in and that he would probably be scarred for life. Emily had to find the man who'd almost ruined her brother's life. She couldn't imagine what kind of monster would sell a sixteen-year-old a gun—a defective gun, at that.

Her parents refused to take the matter to the police. Luckily, John had only been using the gun for target practice, so no one even knew he had the thing. And more important, no one else had been hurt. When she thought about what could have happened, the consequences...

But that was history. Now all she could do was make certain that the same man didn't continue selling guns to kids. She had no compunction about going to the police once she had solid evidence, enough that she didn't have to involve her brother.

Her parents would never forgive her if she sullied the family name. Again.

Her heart raced, climbing into her throat to choke her when the officer—obviously *not* an officer—started toward her. She couldn't take her eyes off his bare, hairbrushed chest, his long, naked thighs. The way the shiny black briefs cupped him... Oh God, it was getting warm in here...

Well-bred ladies most definitely did not react this way!

There were social standards to uphold, a certain degree of expected poise... The litany she'd been reciting to herself came to a screeching halt as the man stopped in front of her.

His eyes, a fierce green, reflected the spotlight. He stared directly at her, then moved so close she could smell the clean male fragrance of him, could feel his body heat. And God, he was hot.

Panting, Emily realized he was waiting for her to give him money. Of all the insane notions...but there were numerous dollars sticking out of those small briefs, and she knew, with unwavering instinct, he wouldn't budge until she'd done as he silently demanded.

Blindly, unable to pull her gaze away, she fumbled in the huge pockets of her worn coat until her fist closed on a bill. She stuck out her hand, offering the money to him.

Wicked was the only way to describe his smile. With a small, barely discernible motion, he shook his head. She dropped her gaze for an instant to where his briefs held all the cash. She'd watched the women put the money there, trying to touch him, but he'd eluded their grasping hands. He'd played up to the audience, getting only close enough to collect a few dollars, then dancing away.

She didn't want to touch him.

Oh, what a lie! She wanted to touch him, all right, but she wouldn't, not here in front of an audience, not ever. She was a respectable lady, she was... She squeaked, leaning back on her seat as he put one hand on the light frame over the bar, the other beside her on the bar stool. She was caged in, unable to breathe. She could see the light sheen of sweat caught in his chest hair, see the small, dark tuft of fine hair under his arm. It seemed almost indecent, and somehow very personal, to see his armpit.

Her body throbbed with heat, and she couldn't swallow. He stood there, demanding, insistent, so very carefully, using only her fingertips, she tucked the bill into his shorts. She registered warm, taut skin, and a sprinkling of crisp hair.

Still holding her gaze, he smiled, his eyes narrowing only the slightest bit. He leaned down next to her face, then placed a small, chaste kiss on her cheek. It had been whisper-light, almost not there, but so potent she felt herself close to fainting.

The audience screamed, loving it, loving him. He laughed, his expression filled with satisfaction, then went back to his dancing. Women begged for the same attention he'd given her, but he didn't comply. Emily figured one pawn in the audience was enough.

Though his focus was now directed elsewhere, it still took Emily several minutes to calm her galloping heartbeat. She continued to watch him, and that kept her tense, because despite everything she'd been brought up to believe, the man excited her.

His dark hair, long in the back, was damp with sweat and beginning to curl. With each movement he made, his shoulders flexed, displaying well-defined muscles and sinew. His backside, held tight in the black briefs, was trim and taut. And his thighs, so long and well-sculpted, looked like the legs of an athlete.

His face was beautiful, almost too beautiful. It was the kind of face that should make innocent women wary of losing their virtue. Green eyes, framed by deliciously long dark lashes and thick eyebrows, held cynical humor and were painfully direct and probing when he chose to use them that way. His nose was straight and narrow, his jaw firm.

Emily realized she was being fanciful, and silently gathered her thoughts. She needed to concentrate on what she'd come to do—finding the gun dealer. According to her brother, who at sixteen had no business hanging out in this part of town, he'd bought the gun on this street. It had been a shady trade-off from the start, cash for the illegal weapon. But John was in a rebellious stage, and his companions of late had ranged from minor gang members to very experienced young ladies. Emily prayed she could help him get back on the straight and narrow, that he could find his peace on an easier road than she'd taken. When she thought of the scars he'd have to live with, the regrets, she knew, deep in her heart, the only way to give him that peace was to find enough evidence to put the gun dealer away.

Though Emily planned to change his mind, John thought his life was over. What attractive, popular teenager could handle the idea of going through life with his face scarred? Then she thought of other kids—kids who might buy a duplicate of the same gun; kids who might be blinded rather than scarred. Or worse. The way the gun had exploded, it could easily have killed someone. And despite her parents' wishes, Emily couldn't stand back and allow that to happen. Her conscience wouldn't allow it.

The show finally ended, the music fading with the lighting until the floor was in darkness. The applause was deafening. And seconds later, the officer was back, his leather jacket slung over his shoulder, his pants and boots in his hand. He thanked the bartender, then took Emily's arm without any explanation, and rapidly pulled her toward an inside door. They narrowly missed the mob of advancing women.

Emily wanted to run, but she'd never in her life resorted to such a display. Besides, now that she knew he wasn't really a policeman, a plan was forming in her mind.

He pulled her into a back room, shut the door, then flipped on a light switch. Emily found herself in a storage closet of sorts, lined with shelves where cleaning supplies sat and a smelly mop tainted the air. A leather satchel rested in the corner. He didn't bother dressing. Instead, he tossed his clothes to the side and moved to stand a hairbreadth away from her.

"You gave me a fifty."

Emily blinked. His words were nowhere near what she'd expected to hear. She tucked in her chin. "I beg your pardon?"

He pulled the cash from his briefs, stacking the bills together neatly in his large hands. "You gave me a fifty-dollar bill. I hadn't realized my show was quite that good."

A fifty! Oh, Lord, Emily. She had no intention of telling him it hadn't been deliberate, that she'd been unable to pull her gaze away from him long enough to find the proper bills. What she'd given him was part of the money earmarked for buying information.

Maybe she could still do that.

Shrugging, she forced her eyes away from his body and stared at the dingy mop. "Since you're not a law enforcement officer, I was hoping the money would...entice you to help me."

He snorted, not buying her line for a second. Emily was relieved he was gentleman enough not to say so.

He gave her a look that curled her toes, then asked, "What kind of *help* do you need, lady?"

It was unbelievably difficult to talk with him so near, and so nearly naked. He smelled delicious, of warm, damp male flesh, though she tried her best not to notice. But his body was too fine to ignore for long, despite her resolve not to give in to unladylike tendencies—such as overwhelming lust—ever again.

She licked her dry lips, then met his eyes. His gaze lingered on her mouth, then slowly coasted over the rest of her body. She knew she wasn't particularly attractive. She had pondered many disguises for this night, disguises ranging anywhere from that of a frumpy homeless lady, to a streetwalker. Somehow, she couldn't imagine herself making a convincing hooker. She was slight of build and her body had never quite...bloomed, as she'd always hoped for. She did, however, think she made an adequate transient.

She cleared her throat. Stiffening her spine, which already felt close to snapping, she said, "I need information."

"Your little trio of drunks didn't tell you enough?"

Since he appeared to have guessed her mission, she didn't bother denying it. "No. They didn't really know anything. And I had to be careful. They didn't seem all that trustworthy. But it's imperative I find out some facts. You...you seem well acquainted with the area?"

She'd said it as a question, and he answered with a nod.

"Good. I want to know of anyone who's selling guns."

He closed his eyes, his mouth twisting in an ironic smirk. "Guns? Just like that, you want to know who's dealing in guns? God, lady, you look like you could go to the nearest reputable dealer and buy any damn thing you wanted." He took a step closer, reaching out his hand to flip a piece of her hair. "I don't know who you thought you'd fool, but you walk like money, talk like money...hell, you even smell like money. What is it? The thrill of going slumming that has you traipsing around here dressed in that getup?"

Emily sucked in her breath at his vulgar question and felt her temper rise. "You have fifty dollars of my money. The least you can do is behave in a civilized, polite manner."

"Wrong." He stepped even closer, the dark, sweat-damp hair on his chest nearly brushing against the tip of her nose. He had to bend low to look her in the eyes, but he managed. "The least I can do is steer your fancy little tail back where you belong. Go home, little girl. Get your thrills somewhere else, somewhere where it's safe."

Suffused with heat at both his nearness and his derisive attitude, it was all Emily could do to keep from cowering. She clicked her teeth together, then swallowed hard. "You don't want to help me. Fine. I'm certain I'll find someone else who will. After all, I'm willing to pay a thousand dollars." Then, turning to make a grand exit, certain she'd made him sorry over losing out on so much money, she said over her shoulder, "I imagine I'll find someone much more agreeable than you within the hour. Goodbye."

There was a split second of stunned silence, then an explosive curse, and Emily decided good breeding could take second place to caution. She reached for the door and almost had it open, when his large hand landed on the wood with a loud crack, slamming it shut again. His warm, hard chest pressed to her back, pinning her to the door. She could barely move; she could barely breathe.

Then his lips touched her ear, whisper-soft, and he said, "You're not going anywhere, sweetheart."

2

SHE FELT light-headed, but she summoned a cool smile.
He was deliberately trying to frighten her—she didn't
know how she knew that, but she was certain of it.
Slowly turning in what little space he allowed her, Emily faced him, her chin held high. "Would you mind
giving me a little breathing room, please?"

"I might."

Might mind, or might move? Emily shook her head.
"You have a rather nasty habit of looming over me,
Mr....?"

For a moment, he remained still and silent, then
thankfully, he took two steps back. He looked at her as
if she might not be entirely sane. Emily stuck out her
hand. "I'm Emily Cooper."

His gaze dropped to her hand, then with a resigned
look of disgust, he enfolded her small hand in his much
larger one, pumping it twice before abruptly releasing
her. He stared at the ceiling. "Judd Sanders."

"It's very nice to meet you, Mr. San—"

"Judd will do." He shook his head, and his gaze came
back to her face. "Look, lady, you can't just come to this
part of town and start waving money around. You'll get

yourself dragged into a dark alley and mugged, possibly raped. Or worse."

Emily wondered what exactly could be worse than being mugged and raped in a dark alley, but she didn't bother asking him. She felt certain he'd come up with some dire consequence to frighten her.

He was watching her closely, and she tried to decide if it was actual concern she saw on his face. She liked to think so. Things still didn't fit. He didn't seem any more suited to this part of town than she did, regardless of his crude manners and bossy disposition.

But now that he'd backed up and given her some room, she was able to think again. "I made certain to stay in front of the stores and in plain sight at all times. If mischief had started, someone surely would have offered assistance." Her eyebrows lifted and she smiled. "You did."

He muttered under his breath, and pointed an accusing finger at her. "You're a menace."

Glaring at him wouldn't get her anywhere, she decided. She needed help, that much was obvious. And who better to help her than a man who evidently knew his way around this part of town, and was well acquainted with its inhabitants. She cleared her throat. "I realize I don't entirely understand how things should be done. Although I'm familiar with the neighborhood, since I work in the soup kitchen twice a week..." She hesitated, then added, "I bought this coat from one of the ladies who comes in regularly. On her, it looked authentic enough. That was even her bag I carried—"

"Miss Cooper."

He said her name in a long, drawn-out sigh. Emily cleared her throat again, then laced her fingers together. "Anyway, while I know the area, at least during the day, I'm not at all acquainted with the workings of the criminal mind. That's why, as I said, I'd like to hire you."

"Because you think *I* do understand the criminal mind?"

"I meant no insult." She felt a little uncertain with him glaring at her like that. "I did get the impression you could handle yourself in almost any situation. Look at how well you took care of those drunkards? You didn't even get bruised, and there were three of them."

"Yeah. But you'd already laid one of them low."

She could feel the blush starting at her hairline and traveling down to cover her entire face. "Yes, well..."

He seemed to give up. One minute he was rigid, his posture so imposing she had to use all her willpower not to cower. Then suddenly, he was idly rubbing his forehead. "Let's get out of here and you can tell me exactly what you want."

Oh, no. She wouldn't tell him that, because what she wanted from him and what was proper were two very different things. But she forgave herself the mental transgression. No woman could possibly be in the same room with this man without having a few fantasies wing through her mind.

Trying for some vagrant humor to lighten his sour mood, she asked, "Wouldn't you like to change first?"

Staring at her, his jaw worked as if he was grinding his teeth. Then he gave one brisk nod. "Turn your head."

Emily blinked. "Turn my... Now wait just a minute! I'll go out to the bar and—"

"No way. I can't trust you not to disappear. Just turn around and stare at the door. I'll only be a minute."

"But I'll know what you're doing!"

He smirked, that was the only word for it. "What's the matter, honey? You afraid you won't be able to resist peeking, knowing I'll be buck naked?"

That was a pretty accurate guess. Emily shook her head. "Don't be ridiculous. It just isn't right, that's all."

"Afraid one of your society friends might meander along and catch you doing something naughty?" He snorted. "Trust me. Not too many upper-crust types visit this part of town. You won't catch yourself in the middle of a scandal."

But she had been caught once, and it had been the most humiliating experience of her life. She'd been alienated from her family ever since.

She thought of that horrid man and nearly cringed. She'd thought herself so above her parents, so understanding of the underprivileged. And she still believed that way. A gentleman was a gentleman, no matter his circumstances. Decency wasn't something that could be bought. But the man who had swept her off her feet, shown her passion and excitement, had proven himself to be anything but decent.

She'd nearly married him before she'd realized he

only wanted her money. Not her. Never her. He'd used her, used her family, made a newsworthy pest of himself, and her parents had never forgiven her for it.

She could still hear herself trying to explain her actions. But her mother believed a lady didn't involve herself in such situations, under any circumstances.

A lady never lost her head to something as primal as lust.

Lifting her chin, Emily gave Judd the frostiest stare she could devise. "I can most certainly control myself." Then she turned her back on him. "Go right ahead, Mr. Sanders. But please make it quick. It is getting rather late."

Emily heard him chuckling, heard the rustle of clothing, and she held her breath. It was only a matter of a minute and a half before he told her she could turn around.

Very slowly, just in case he was toying with her, Emily peered at him. He was dressed in jeans, and had pulled on a flannel shirt. He was sitting on a crate, tugging on low boots. When he stood to fasten his shirt, Emily noticed he hadn't yet done up his jeans. She tried not to blush, but it was a futile effort.

He ignored her embarrassment. "So, Emily. Where exactly are you from?"

Her gaze was on his hands as he shoved his shirttails into his pants. "The Crystal Lakes area," she said. "And you?"

He gave a low, soft whistle. "The Crystal Lakes? Damn. No kidding?"

Annoyed, she finally forced her attention to his face. "I certainly wouldn't lie about it."

He took her arm and led her out of the storeroom. He had stuffed his dance props into the leather satchel he carried in his other hand. "I'll bet you live in a big old place with plenty of rooms, don't you?"

Emily eyed him with a wary frown. She wasn't certain how much she should tell him about herself. "I have enough space, I suppose."

He asked abruptly, "How did you get here?"

"Actually, I took the bus. I didn't think parking my car here would be such a good idea."

"No doubt. What do you drive, anyway? A Rolls?"

"Of course not."

"So?" He pulled her out the door and into the brisk night. "What do you tool around in?"

"Tool around? I drive a Saab."

"Ah."

"What does that mean? Ah?" He was moving her along again, treating her like a dog on a leash. And with his long-legged stride, it was all she could do to keep up. He stopped near a back alley, and Emily realized they were at the rear of the bar. "Why didn't we just go out the back door instead of walking all the way around?"

"'Ah' means your choice of transportation shouldn't surprise me. And we came this way so I could spare you from being harassed. Believe me, the men working in the back would have a field day with an innocent like you."

Don't ask. Don't ask. "What makes you believe I'm an innocent?"

Judd opened the door to a rusty, disreputable pickup truck and motioned for her to get inside. She hesitated, suddenly not certain she should trust him.

But he only stood there, watching her with that intense, probing green gaze. Finally, Emily grabbed the door frame to hoist herself inside.

Judd shook his head. "And you ask how I know you're an innocent?"

Before Emily could reply, he slammed the door and walked around to get in behind the wheel. "Buckle up."

She watched his profile as he steered the truck out of the alley and onto the main road. The lights from well-spaced street lamps flashed across his features. Trying to avoid staring at him, she looked around the truck and she saw a strip of delicate black lace draped over the rearview mirror.

Judd noticed her fascination with the sheer lace and grinned. "A memento of my youth."

Trying for disinterest, Emily muttered, "Really."

"I was sixteen, she was eighteen."

Sixteen. The same age as her brother—and obviously into as much mischief as John.

Judd ran his fingers down the lace as if in fond memory. "We were in such a hurry, we ripped her panties getting them off." He flashed her a grin. "Black lace still makes me crazy."

Emily went perfectly quiet, then tightly crossed her legs. *There's no way he can know what your panties look like,*

Emily, she told herself. But still, she made an effort to bring the conversation back to her purpose. She had to find a way to help John.

Reminded of the reason she was with Judd in the first place, Emily turned to him. Taking a deep breath, she said, "I need to find out who's selling semiautomatic weapons to kids. I...I know a boy who had one blow up in his face. He was badly injured. Luckily, no one else was around."

The truck swerved, and Judd shot her a look that could have cut ice. *"Blew up?"*

His tone was harsh, and Emily couldn't help huddling closer against her door. "Yes. He very nearly lost an eye."

Judd muttered a curse, but when he glanced at her again, his expression was carefully controlled. "Did you go to the police?"

"I can't." She tightened her lips, feeling frustrated all over again. "The boy's parents won't allow him to be implicated. They refuse to realize just how serious this situation is. They have money, so they took him out of the country to be treated. They won't return until they're certain he's safe."

"Yeah. A lot of parents believe bad things will go away if you ignore them. Unfortunately, that's not true. But Emily, you have to know, there's nothing you can do to stop the crime on these streets. The drugs, the gangs and the selling of illegal arms, it'll go on forever."

"I refuse to believe that!" She turned in her seat, taking her frustration out on him. "I have to do something.

Maybe I can figure out a way to stop this guy who sold that gun. If everyone would get involved—"

Judd laughed, cutting her off. "Like the folks who whisked their baby boy out of the country? How old was this kid, anyway? Old enough to know better, I'll bet." He shook his head, giving her a look that blatantly called her a fool. "Don't waste your time. Go back to your rich neighborhood, your fancy car and your fancier friends. Let the cops take care of things."

She was so angry, she nearly cried. It had always been that way. She never shed a tear over pain or hurt feelings, but let her get really mad, and she bawled like an infant. His attitude toward her brother infuriated her.

Judd stopped at a traffic light, and she jerked her door open, trying to step out. His long hard fingers immediately wrapped around her upper arm, preventing her from leaving.

"What the hell do you think you're doing?"

"Let me go." She was proud of her feral tone. "Did you hear me? Get your hands off me." She struggled, pulling against his hold.

"Dammit! Get back in this truck!"

The light had changed and the driver of the car behind them blasted his horn. "I've changed my mind, Mr. Sanders," she told him. "I no longer require your help. I'll find someone else, someone who won't choose to ridicule me every other second."

He peered at her closely, then sighed. "Aw, hell. Don't tell me you're going to cry."

"No, I am not going to cry!" But she could feel the tears stinging her eyes, which angered her all the more. How could she have been so wrong about him—and he so wrong about her? She didn't have fancy friends; she didn't have any friends. Most of the time, she didn't have anybody—except her brother. She loved him dearly, and John trusted her. When the rest of her family had turned their backs on her, her brother had been there for her, making her laugh, giving her the support she needed to get through it all.

She couldn't let him down now, even if he didn't realize he needed her help. He was the only loving family she could claim, the only one who still cared about her, despite her numerous faults. And she knew, regardless of the gun incident, John was a good person.

Several cars were blaring their horns now, and Judd yanked her back inside, retaining his hold as he moved out of the stream of traffic and over to the curb. He didn't release her. "Look, I'm sorry. Don't go and get weepy on me, okay?"

"You, Mr. Sanders, are an obnoxious ass!" Emily jerked against him, but he held firm. "I always cry when I'm angry."

"Well...don't be angry then."

Unbelievable. The man had been derisive, insulting and arrogant from the moment she'd met him, but now his tone had changed to a soft, gentle rebuke. He had a problem with female tears? She almost considered giving in to a real tantrum just to make him suffer, but that had never been her way. The last thing she wanted from Judd was pity.

"Ignore me," she muttered, feeling like a fool. "It's been a trying week. But I am determined to see this thing through. I'll find the man who sold that gun. I have a plan, a very solid plan. I could certainly use your help, but if you're only going to be nasty, I believe I'd rather just find someone else."

JUDD WAS AMAZED by her speech. Then his eyes narrowed. No way in hell was he going to let her run loose. She was a menace. She was a pain.

She was unbelievably innocent and naive.

Judd shook his head, then steered the truck back into the street. "Believe me, lady. I'm about as nice as you're going to find in these parts. Besides, I think I might be interested in your little plan, after all. I mean, what the hell? A thousand bucks is a thousand bucks. That was the agreed amount, right?"

Emily nodded.

Lifting one shoulder, Judd said, "Can't very well turn down money like that."

"No. No, I wouldn't think so." She watched him warily, and Judd thought, what the hell? It would be easier to work with her, than around her. If he turned her down, she'd only manage to get in his way, or get herself hurt. That was such a repugnant thought, he actually groaned.

He'd have to keep his cool, maintain his cover, and while he was at it, he could keep an eye on her. Maybe he could pretend to help her, but actually steer her far enough away from the trouble that she wouldn't be any problem at all.

Yeah, right.

It would probably be better to try to convince her to give up her ridiculous plan first. He glanced at her, saw the rigid way she held herself, and knew exactly how to dissuade her. "There are a few conditions we should discuss."

Emily heaved a deep breath. "Conditions?"

"Yeah. The money's great. But I'll still have to work nights at the bar. Actually, only Tuesdays and Thursdays. *Ladies'* nights."

Emily hastened to reassure him. "I don't have a problem with that. I wouldn't want to interfere with your...career."

His laugh was quick and sharp, then he shook his head. "Right. My career." He glanced at her again, grinning, wondering if she could possibly realize how uncomfortable he was with that particular career. "That's not the only thing, though."

"There's something else?"

"Yeah. You see, we'll need a place to meet. Neutral ground and all that. Someplace away from prying eyes."

Emily stared.

"You stand out like a sore thumb, honey. We can't just have you traipsing around in that neighborhood. People will wonder what you're up to. It could blow the whole thing."

"I see."

"My apartment is close to here. No one would pay any attention to you coming in or out. It wouldn't even matter what time we met. We'll need to work closely together, finesse these plans of yours. What d'ya say?"

Her mouth opened, but all that came out was, "Oh God."

Lifting one dark eyebrow, Judd felt triumphant. She was already realizing the implications of spending so much time alone with him. He hid his relief and said, "Come again?"

Emily shook her head, then at the same time said, "Yes, that is...I suppose..." She heaved a sigh, straightened her back, and then nodded. "Okay."

Judd stared at her, trying not to show his disbelief. "What do you mean, okay?" He'd thought for certain, since everything else had failed, that this would send her running. But no. She seemed to like the damn idea. She was actually smiling now.

"I mean, if you think we could successfully operate from your apartment, I'll agree to meet you there."

Contrary female. "Emily..." He faltered. He liked saying her name, liked how it sounded, all fresh and pure. She looked at him, with those huge, doe eyes steady on his face. She was too trusting. She was a danger to herself. If he didn't keep close tabs on her, she'd end up in trouble. He was sure of it.

"You were going to say something, Mr. Sanders?"

Nothing she would like hearing. He shook his head. "Just be quiet and let me think."

Obediently, she turned away and stared out her window. He wasn't buying her compliance for a minute. He had a gut feeling there wasn't an obedient bone in her slim body. He also suspected she was as stubborn as all hell, once she'd set her mind on something. And she was set to find a gun dealer.

The truck was heating up. It was late spring and even though the nights were still a little chilly, the days were warming up into the seventies. Without any fanfare, and apparently trying not to draw undue attention to herself, Emily began unbuttoning the oversize coat. Judd watched from the corner of his eye.

Just to razz her, because she took the bait so easily, he asked, "Would you like me to give you a drumroll?"

She turned to face him. "I beg your pardon?"

She looked honestly confused. He tried to hide his grin. "Every good striptease needs music."

"I'm not stripping!"

He shrugged, amused by the blush on her cheeks that was visible even in the dark interior of the truck. She was apparently unused to masculine teasing, maybe even to men in general.

He snorted at his own foolishness. It was men like himself, coarse and inelegant, that she wasn't used to. He imagined she had plenty of sophisticated guys clamoring for her attention. And that fact nettled him, even though it shouldn't. Grumbling, he said, "You should try it. Everyone should experience stripping just once. It's a rush."

She held her coat together with clenched fingers, her

look incredulous. If she knew him better, she'd know what a lie he'd just told. He hated taking off his clothes in front of so many voracious women. But she didn't know him, and most likely never would. He should keep that fact in mind before he did something stupid. *Like what, you idiot? Like promising you'd take care of her gun dealer for her, so she could take her cute little backside and big brown eyes back home where it's safe?* No, he most definitely couldn't do that, no matter how much he'd like to.

They came to the entrance to Crystal Lakes. "Which way?"

He'd startled her. She'd practically jumped out of her seat, and he was left wondering exactly where her mind had been. "Which way to your place? You didn't think I'd take you to my apartment tonight, did you? In case you haven't noticed, lady, it's after midnight. And I've put in a full day. Tomorrow will be soon enough."

The truck was left to idle while they stared at each other. Finally in a small voice filled with suspicion, Emily said, "You're not just getting rid of me, are you? You'll really help me?"

Those eyes of hers could be lethal. He wanted nothing more than to tug her close and promise her he wouldn't leave her, that he'd take care of everything, that he'd... She looked so damn vulnerable. It didn't make a bit of sense. Usually people with big money went around feeling confident that money would get them anything. They didn't bother with doubts.

Irritated now, he rubbed the bridge of his nose, then

said in a low tone, "Since I haven't gotten my thousand bucks yet, you can be sure I'll be sticking around."

After heaving a small sigh, she said, "Of course."

Now, why did she have to sound so disappointed? And why did he feel like such a jerk?

"Left, up the hill, then the first street on the right."

Judd knew he had no business forming fantasies over a woman who blushed every time she spoke. Especially since he'd have to keep her close, more to protect her than anything else. She didn't understand the magnitude of what she was tampering with, the lethal hold gun dealers had on the city.

An idea had been forming in his mind ever since he'd realized he couldn't discourage her from trying to save the world. He'd thought, if he became aggressive enough, she'd run back home to safety.

Instead, she'd only threatened to find someone else to help her. And he couldn't let that happen. She might get herself killed, or maybe she'd actually find out something and inadvertently get in the way. He'd worked too hard for that to happen. He wouldn't allow anything—or anyone—to interfere. He *would* get the bastard who'd shot Max. But damn, he'd never expected Emily to openly accept his plans.

Crystal Lakes, as exclusive and ritzy as it was, sat only about twenty-five minutes from the lower east side. It was one of those areas where you could feel the gradual change as you left hell and entered heaven. The grass started looking greener, the business district slipped away, and eventually everything was clean and untainted.

Emily pointed out her house, a large white Colonial, with a huge front porch. It looked as if it had been standing there for more than a hundred years, and was surprisingly different from the newer, immense homes recently built in the area.

There were golden lights in every window, providing a sense of warmth. A profusion of freshly planted spring flowers surrounded the perimeter, and blooming dogwoods randomly filled the yard. All in all, the place was very impressive, but not quite what he'd expected. Somehow, he'd envisioned her stationed in real money. Any truly successful businessperson could afford this house.

Judd stared around the isolated grounds. "Do you live here by yourself?"

She nodded, not quite looking at him, her hands clasped nervously in her lap.

"No husband or little ones to help fill up the space?"

"No. No husband. No children."

"Why not? I thought all debutantes were married off at an early age."

He didn't think she'd answer at first, but then she licked her lips and her skittish gaze settled on his face. "I was...engaged once. But things didn't work out." She rushed through her words, seemingly unable to stop herself. "I bought this house about a year ago. My parents don't particularly like it—it's one of the smaller homes in the community. But it was an original estate, not one built when the Lakes was developed. It's been renovated, and I think it's charming."

She said the words defensively, as if she expected some scathing comment from him. Judd didn't like being affected this way, but there was something about Emily that touched him. He could *feel* her emotions, had been feeling them since first making eye contact with her. And right now, she seemed almost wounded.

Very gently, he asked, "Did you see to the renovations yourself?"

"Yes."

He looked around the dark, secluded yard and shook his head. "Your parents approve of your living here alone?"

"No, but it doesn't matter what they think. When my grandmother died, she left me a large inheritance. My parents expected me to buy a condo near them and then invest the rest using their suggestions." Her hands tightened in her lap and she swallowed. "But I loved this house on sight. I'd already planned to buy it, and receiving the inheritance let me do so sooner than I'd planned. I don't regret a single penny I spent on the place. Everything is just as I want it."

"What if you hadn't gotten the inheritance?"

"I would have found a job. I'm educated. I'm not helpless." She gave him a narrow-eyed look. "But this way, I don't have to. I'm financially independent."

And alone. "How old are you, Emily?"

She raised her chin, a curious habit he'd noticed she used whenever she felt threatened. "Thirty."

He couldn't hide his surprise. "You don't look more than twenty." Without thinking, he reached out and touched her cheek, his fingertips drifting over her fine, porcelain skin. "Twenty and untouched."

She jerked away. "Are we going to sit in the driveway all night? Go around the back, to the kitchen door."

He shouldn't let her give him orders, but what the hell. He put the truck in gear and did as directed.

The darkness of the hour had hidden quite a few things. There was a small lake behind her property, pretty with the moon reflecting off its surface. Of course, there were some twenty such lakes in the Crystal Lakes community, so he shouldn't have been surprised.

"Is the lake stocked?"

"Yes. But it's seldom used. Occasionally, one or two of the neighborhood children come here to fish. My lake is the most shallow, so it's the safest. And it's the only one on this side of the community. Most of the lakes are farther up."

"You don't mind the kids trampling around your yard?"

"Of course not. They're good kids. They usually feed the ducks and catch a frog or two. I enjoy watching them."

Judd stared back at the house. There was a large window that faced the backyard and the lake. He could picture her sitting there, content to watch the children play. Maybe longing for things she didn't have. Things money couldn't buy.

Hell, he was becoming fanciful.

Disgusted with himself, knowing he'd been away from normal society too long and that was probably the reason she seemed so appealing, he parked the truck and got out. The fresh air cleared his head.

He opened Emily's door to help her out, but she held back, watching him nervously. "I'll make sure you get inside okay, then I'll take off. We can hook up again tomorrow morning."

"Oh. Yes. That will be fine."

She sounded relieved that he didn't intend to come inside tonight, and perversely, he changed his mind. He'd come in, all right, but with his imagination so active, he couldn't trust himself to be alone with her any length of time. Anyway, he told himself, she wasn't his type—not even close. She was much too small and frail. He liked his women big, with bountiful breasts and lush hips.

As far as he could tell, Emily didn't have a figure.

But those eyes... She walked up a small, tidy patio fronted by three shallow steps, then unlocked the back door and flipped a switch. Bright fluorescent light cascaded through a spotless kitchen and spilled outside onto the patio. Judd saw flowerpots everywhere, filled with spring flowers, and a small outdoor seating group arranged to his right. Everything seemed cheery and colorful...like a real home, and not at all what he'd expected.

Damn, he'd have to find some way to dissuade her from her plan before he got in over his head.

She turned and gave him a small, uncertain smile. "About tomorrow..."

He interrupted her, coming up the three steps and catching her gaze. "Let's make sure we understand each other, Emily, so there won't be any mistakes."

She nodded, and he deliberately stepped closer, watching with satisfaction as she tried to pull back, even though there was no place to go. Good, he thought. At least she had some sense of self-preservation.

He braced his hands on the door frame, deliberately looming over her. "From this second on, I call the shots, with no arguments from you. If you really want my help, you'll do as I tell you, whatever I tell you." He waited until she'd backed all the way into the kitchen, then he added, "You understand all that?"

3

EMILY'S MOUTH opened twice, but nothing came out. She was too stunned to think rationally, too appalled to react with any real thought. Judd dropped his arms and stepped completely into the kitchen, watching her, and by reflex alone, she started sidling toward the hall door. She had made a terrible mistake. Her instincts had been off by a long shot.

Judd's smile was pure wickedness. "Where ya' goin', Emily?"

"I, ah, I just thought of something…"

Like a loud blast, his laugh erupted, filling the silence of the kitchen.

She halted, a spark of suspicion beginning to form. "*What* is so funny?"

"The look on your face. Did you think I had visions of taking you instead of the money?" He shook his head, and Emily felt her cheeks flame. He was still chuckling when he said, "It only makes sense that I'd be in charge—after all, that's what you'll be paying me for. Like I told you, a rich little lady like yourself would only draw a lot of unnecessary attention hanging around that area. You'll have to follow my lead, and do as I tell you if you want to stay safe. And another thing, we need to figure out some reason for you being there at all. I think we'll have to do a little acting. Your part will be easy, since you'll just be the rich lady. That leaves me as the kept man." He spread his arms wide. "As far as everyone will be concerned, I'm yours. There's no other reason why a woman like you would be around a man like me, unless she was slumming. So that's the reason we'll use."

She was so mortified, she wanted to die. Stiff-backed, she turned away from him and walked over to lean against the tiled counter near the sink. She heard Judd close the door, and seconds later, his hands landed on her shoulders, holding her firm.

"Don't get all huffy now. We have things to discuss. Serious things."

"You mean, you don't intend to taunt me anymore? My goodness, how gracious."

"You've got a real smart mouth, don't you? No, don't answer that. I'm sorry I teased you, but I couldn't resist. You're just too damn easy to fluster." He turned her to face him, then tipped up her chin.

"Here, now, don't go blushing again. Not that you don't look cute when you do, but I really think we should talk."

Emily stepped carefully away, not wanting him to know how his nearness, his touch, affected her. Even after all his taunting, she still went breathless and too warm inside when he was close. And ridiculously, it angered her when he belittled himself, claiming she could have no interest in him other than as a sex partner. The physical appeal was there, but it was more than that. Much more. He had helped her. He'd actually taken on three inebriated men to protect her, even though he wasn't a real cop. And he was willing to help her again. She discounted the money; what she was asking could put his life at risk. He must be motivated by more than money to get involved.

But for now, she couldn't sort it all out. Especially not with her senses still rioting at his nearness. She drew a deep breath, then let it out again. "I thought we were going to wait until morning to make any plans. It is getting rather late."

"No, I've decided it can't wait. But I won't keep you long. Pull up a chair and get comfortable."

Emily didn't particularly want to get comfortable, but she also didn't want to risk driving Judd away. For the moment, he was the best hope she had of ever finding the man who'd sold her brother the gun. She knew her limitations, and fitting in around the lower east side of Springfield was probably the biggest of them. She needed him.

As she headed for a chair, Judd caught the back of her coat, drawing her up short. "It's warm in here. Why don't you take this off?"

He was watching her closely again, and she couldn't fathom his thoughts. She shrugged, then started to slip the shabby wool coat from her shoulders. Judd's eyes went immediately to the tiny camera she wore on a strap around her neck.

"What the hell is that?"

She jumped, then lost her temper with his barking tone. "Will you please quit cursing at me!"

He seemed stunned by her outburst, but he did nod. "Answer me."

"It's rather obviously a camera."

Closing his eyes and looking as though he were involved in deep prayer, Judd said, "Please tell me you weren't taking pictures tonight."

"No. I didn't take any." She lifted her chin, knowing what his reaction would be, then added, "Tonight."

"You just had to clarify that, didn't you, before I could really relax." His sigh was long and drawn out, then he led her to the polished pine table sitting in the middle of her quarry-stone kitchen floor. He pulled out a chair for her, silently insisting that she sit. "So when did you take pictures?"

"I've been checking that area for three nights now." She ignored his wide-eyed amazement, and his muttered cursing. "The first night, I took some shots of things that didn't look quite right. You know, groups of men who were huddled together talking. Cars that were parked where they probably shouldn't be. Things like that. Not that I really suspected them of anything. But I didn't want to come home empty-handed.

"I was hoping to find something concrete tonight, so I brought the camera again. Let's face it. If I did find out anything, I doubt the police would simply take my word for it. I mean, if they were at all concerned with that awful man who's selling defective guns, well...they'd be doing something right now." Judd cringed, but Emily rushed on. "If I had something on film, I'd have solid evidence. The police would have to get involved. But there wasn't anything incriminating."

Judd's mouth was tight and his eyes grew more narrow with each word she spoke. "You've been hanging out in the lower east side for three days...rather, nights?"

"Yes."

His palm slapped the table and he leaned forward to loom over her again, caging her in her chair. Emily slid back in her seat, stunned by his fury. And he *was* furious, she had no doubt of that.

"Never again, you got that!" He was so close, his breath hit her face in hot gusts. "From this day on, you don't even think about going anywhere, especially to the lower east side, without me. Ever. You got that?"

Emily bolted upright, forcing him to move away so they wouldn't smack noses. "You don't give me orders, Mr. Sanders!"

"Judd, dammit," he said, now sounding merely disgruntled. "I told you to call me Judd."

"I hired you, *Judd*, not the other way around."

He grabbed her shoulders and pushed her into her seat. His tone was lower, but no less firm. "I'm serious, Emily. You obviously don't have the sense God gave a goose, and if you want my help on this, I insist you stay in one piece. That won't happen if you go wandering around in areas where you shouldn't be. It's too dangerous. Hell, it's a wonder you've survived as long as you have."

Emily tried to calm herself, but he was so close, she couldn't think straight. She recognized his real concern, something money couldn't possibly buy. Satisfied that her instincts hadn't failed her after all, she tried to re-assure him. Her voice emerged as a whisper. "I have been careful, Judd. I promise. No one saw me take the pictures. But just in case, I took shots of inconsequential things, too. Like the children who were playing in the street, and the vagrant standing on the corner. If anyone saw me, they'd just think I was doing an exposé. They'd be flattered, not concerned."

"You can't know that."

He, too, was easing back, as if suddenly aware of their positions. Slipping the camera off over her head, he said, "I'll take this, in case there is anything impor-tant on the film."

Emily started to object, even though she truly didn't believe she had photographed anything relevant. Then she noticed where his gaze had wandered. Very briefly, his eyes lit on her mouth, then her throat. Emily could feel her pulse racing there.

Still frowning, but also looking a little confused, Judd laid the camera on the table, then caught the lapels of her coat and eased them wide. He just stood there, holding her coat open, looking at her. He didn't move, but his look was so hot, and he was still so near she grew breathless.

She felt choked by the neck of her dress, a high-collared affair that buttoned up the front and was long enough to hang to midcalf. It was sprinkled with small, dainty blue flowers, a little outdated maybe, but she liked it. She'd long ago accepted she had no fashion sense, so she bought what pleased her, not what the designers dictated.

Judd lifted a finger, almost reluctantly, and touched the small blue bow that tied her collar at her throat. She could hear his breathing, could see his intense concentration as he watched the movement of his hand. With a slow, gentle tug, he released the bow, and the pad of his finger touched her warm skin.

Emily parted her lips to breathe. She wasn't thinking about what he was doing or why. She was only feeling, the sensations overwhelming, swamping her senses. She surrendered to them—to Judd—without a whimper, good sense and caution lost in the need to be wanted, to share herself with another person.

Judd lifted his gaze to her face. He searched her expression for a timeless moment, his eyes hard and bright. Then abruptly, he moved away. He stalked to the door, his head down, his hands fisted on his hips.

He inhaled deeply, and Emily watched the play of muscles across his back. "I want your promise, Emily. I don't want you to make a single move without me."

Gruff and low, it took a second for his words to filter into her mind. They were so different from her own thoughts, so distant from the mood he'd created. She cleared her throat and tried to clear her mind. Judd still had his back to her, his arms now crossed over his chest. He sounded almost angry, and she didn't understand him. Could he, who barely knew her, truly be so concerned for her well-being? "You'll help me? You're not just putting me off?"

"I'll help. But we move when I say, and not before."

She wished he'd look at her so she could see his face, but he didn't. "Since I assume you know the best time to find information, I'll wait."

Finally, he turned to her. "This house is secure?"

"Very."

He picked up the camera, then opened the door. "I've got to go. I have a few things to do yet. But I want you to promise me you'll stay inside—no more investigating tonight."

Nervously, Emily fingered the loose ties to her bow. She considered retying it, but decided against drawing any further attention to the silly thing. Judd glanced down at her fingers, and his expression hardened. "Promise me you'll stay in your castle, princess. We can talk more in the morning."

"Yes. I won't go anywhere else tonight." She tried to make her tone firm, but some of her fear came through in her next question. "How will I reach you tomorrow?"

Judd stood silently watching her a minute longer. "You got a pen and paper anywhere around here?"

Emily opened a drawer and pulled out a pad and pencil. Judd quickly scrawled several lines. "This is my number at the apartment, and this is the one at the bar. And just in case, here's my address. Now, I mean it, Emily. Don't make a move without me."

She tried not to look too greedy when she snatched the paper out of his hand. "I promise."

He hesitated another moment, then stepped outside, pulling the door shut behind him. Emily watched through the window as his truck drove away, wondering where he was going, but knowing she didn't have the right to ask. Perhaps he had a lady friend waiting on him.

Of course he does, Emily, she told herself. *A man like him probably has dozens of women.* But they're not ladies. He wouldn't want a lady.

And for some reason, that thought sent a small, forbidden thrill curling through her insides.

ANGER AND FRUSTRATION were not a good combination. Judd didn't understand himself. Or more to the point, he didn't understand his reaction to Emily.

He'd been a hairbreadth away from kissing her. Not a sweet little peck. No, he'd wanted his tongue in her mouth, his lips covering hers, feeling her urgency. He'd wanted, dammit, to devour her completely.

And she would have loved it, he could tell that much from her racing pulse and her soft, inviting eyes. She may play the proper little Miss Priss to perfection, but she had fire. Enough to burn him if he let her.

It wasn't the time and she wasn't the person for him to be getting ideas about. But he'd taunted her without mercy, wanting to conquer her, to show her he was male to her female. To prove...what? That he could and would protect her? That he'd solve her problems so she could smile more? He didn't know.

He'd had women, of course, but none that meant anything beyond physical pleasure. None that he'd wanted to claim, to brand in the most primal, basic way. He didn't know what it was, but Emily was simply different. And she affected him differently.

That dress of hers...so feminine, so deceiving. He'd always heard other men joke about having a lady in the parlor and a wanton in the bedroom. The dress had looked innocent enough, but her eyes...

He knew, even though he wasn't happy knowing, that Emily fit the descriptive mix of lady and wanton to a tee. It was an explosive fantasy, the thought of having a woman who would unleash her passion for just one man, that no one would ever guess unless they were with her, covering her, inside her.

Beneath her dress, he could make out the faint, delicate curve of her breasts, her narrow rib cage. She was so slight of build, but so feminine. She had the finest skin he'd ever seen, warm and smooth and pale. And loyalty. She must be damn loyal to this kid—whoever he was—to take such risks for him.

Judd's thighs clenched and his heart raced. He hadn't been able to resist touching her, and she hadn't protested when he did.

She was too trusting for her own good. And he was too intuitive to be fooled by her prissy demeanor. Emily Cooper had more than her fair share of backbone, and that was almost as sexy as her eyes.

Stopping at a corner drugstore and leaving the truck at the curb, Judd got out to use the lighted pay phone. He never used the phone in his apartment to contact headquarters, in case there were prying ears. To his disgust, his hands shook as he fished a quarter out of his jeans pocket. He made the call, and then waited.

Lieutenant Howell picked up on the first ring. "Yeah?"

"Sanders here."

"It's about time. Where the hell have you been?"

Judd closed his eyes, not relishing the chore ahead of him. This wasn't going to be easy. He took a deep breath, then told his boss, "We have a little problem."

"I'm waiting."

"I met a lady tonight."

"Is that supposed to surprise me, Judd? Hell, you're working as a male stripper. I imagine you meet a lot of broads every damn night."

"Not a broad," Judd said, the edge in his tone evident. "A lady. And she was actively looking for Donner, though she hasn't put a name to him yet. Seems she knows a kid who had a faulty automatic blow up in his face, and she's pegged Donner as the seller."

There was a low whistle, then, "No kidding?"

"The kid's alive, but from what I understand, he's in pretty bad shape. His parents have taken him out of the country." Then, in a drier tone, Judd added, "They're upper-league."

Judd expected the cursing, then the inevitable demand for details. The telling took all of three minutes, and during that time, Howell didn't make a single sound. Judd tried to downplay his initial meeting with Emily and the fact she'd seen him perform, but there was no way to get around it completely. When Judd finished, he heard a rough rumble from Howell that could have been either a chuckle or a curse. "She could throw a wrench into the works."

Judd chose his words very carefully. "Maybe not. I've been thinking about it, and it might actually strengthen my case. Being a stripper in such a sleazy joint makes me look pretty unethical. And I've made it known I'd do just about anything, including stripping, to make a fast buck."

"But Donner hasn't taken the bait yet."

"He will." Judd was certain of that. Donner always used available locals. That was how he worked. "It will happen. But maybe, with a classy woman hanging around to make me look all the more unscrupulous, Donner will buy in a little quicker."

"You think he'll figure the little lady is keeping you?"

"What else would he think? We're hardly the perfect couple. As long as she's informed and close enough for me to keep an eye on her, she'll be safe. And Donner will definitely get curious. Besides, I don't have much choice. She made it real plain she'd investigate on her own if I didn't see fit to help her. It's a sure bet she'd tip Donner off and send him running."

Howell chuckled. "Sounds like you got everything nicely under control."

No. He didn't have his libido under control, or his

protective male instincts that had him wanting to look after her despite his obligations to the job and his loyalty to Max. "I can handle things, I think. It would have been better not to have a civilian involved, but my options are limited now."

"I could have her picked up for some trumped-up violation. That might buy you a little time to settle things without her around."

The thought of Emily being humiliated that way, being harassed—by anyone other than himself, was unthinkable. "No. I'll keep an eye on her. Besides, she's so clean, she squeaks. I doubt you'd find anything. And I already tried scaring her off, but she's sticking to her guns."

"Determined, huh?"

Judd snorted. "I almost think she wants Donner as bad as I do. She was taking pictures. Can you imagine? I took the film. I don't think there's anything important on it, but I don't want to take any chances. Not with this case." *And not with her.* "So I'll let her hang around a while, and use the situation to our advantage. In any case, she'll probably be with me when I perform at the bar on Tuesday."

"Keep me posted as soon as you know about the film. And in the meantime, watch your backside. Don't go getting romantic ideas and blow this whole thing."

"Fat chance." He hoped he sounded convincing. "I just wanted you to know what was going on."

"You need any backup on hand, just in case?"

"No." Everything had gone better than he could have

hoped. His performance was convincing, even superior to the other dancers'. But he didn't intend to share all that over the phone. It was humiliating. "I don't want to take a chance on blowing it now. I'm accepted. No one suspects me of being anything but a stripper."

"Yeah, you fit the bill real good."

Judd ignored that taunting comment. They'd checked the place over in minute detail before setting up the stakeout. Donner definitely used the room above the bar to make his deals and meet contacts. So it was imperative that Judd be on hand. Unfortunately, the bar was such a damn landmark, having been there for generations, the only transient positions available were the dancers'. The bartenders had been there for years and the bar's ownership hadn't changed hands except within the same family. If Judd wanted Donner he was stuck stripping. And he wanted Donner real bad.

"As I said, it's a believable cover, but I hope like hell we can wrap it up soon. I don't want to take any unnecessary chances."

And he didn't want Emily to get caught in the middle of his own personal war.

"Judd? Is there something you're not telling me? Has something happened? Is it time?"

His instincts told him things would come to a head soon, but he kept that thought to himself. "Hell, it's past time, but who knows? Something's bound to break soon. Either a deal or my back. Those ladies can be real demanding when you're peeling off your clothes."

As he'd intended, his cryptic complaints lightened

the mood. "You're the perfect guy for the job. Just don't start enjoying yourself and decide to leave us for bigger and better things." Howell laughed, then cleared his throat. "Stay in touch, and for God's sake, stay alert. Get the hell out if things go sour."

"I'll keep my eyes open."

Judd felt a certain finality settle over him as he replaced the receiver. His superior hadn't nixed his plans with Emily, and it was too late to call off the cover, regardless of his personal feelings. He'd be spending a lot of time in Emily's company. And that filled him with both dread and sizzling anticipation.

HE HADN'T SLEPT a wink. The combination of worry and excitement from his vivid dreams of Emily worked to keep him tossing all night. But the knock on the apartment door sounded insistent, so he reluctantly forced himself out from under the sheet, then wrapped it around himself to cover his nudity.

"Just a damn minute!" On his way out of the room, he picked up his watch and saw it was only eight-thirty. Just dandy.

Carrying his pistol, he looked out the peephole, then cursed. He stuck the gun in a drawer, just before jerking the door open. He managed to startle Emily, who nearly dropped a large basket she was holding in both hands. "Are you one of those perverse people who rises with the sun?"

Emily didn't look at his face. She was too busy staring at his body. Judd sighed in disgust. "I'm showing less now than I did last night, and you didn't faint then, so please, pull it together, will ya?"

That moony-eyed look of hers was going to be the death of him. A man could take only so much.

And she was looking especially fetching this morning in some kind of light, spring dress. It was just as concealing as the one she'd worn last night, but there was no tie at her throat, only a pearl brooch that looked as if it cost a small fortune. This dress nipped in at the waist, and showed how tiny she was. He could easily span her waist with his hands. His palms tingled at the thought.

"What the hell are you doing here, Emily? It's still early."

"I...actually, I thought we might have breakfast. You did say we would talk this morning."

"Eager to get started, are you?" Turning away, Judd stared toward the kitchen, then back to Emily. "I wasn't up yet. If you want coffee, you'll have to make it."

Emily seemed to shake herself. "Ah, no. Actually, I thought...you know, to thank you for everything you did for me last night...taking me home and all that, well...I cooked for you."

She ended in a shrug, and Judd realized how embarrassed she was. Or maybe she thought he'd mock her again, ridicule her for her consideration.

He raked a hand through his hair, still holding the sheet with a fist. "What have you got in there?"

He indicated the basket with a toss of his head. Emily's smile was fleeting, and very relieved. She glanced around the room, taking in the apartment's minimal furnishings: a couch, a small table with two chairs, a few lamps, a stereo, but no television. His bedroom sat off to the right, where the open door allowed her to see a small night table and a rumpled bed. The kitchen was merely a room divided by a small, three-foot bar.

He liked the place, even though the neighborhood was rough and the tenants noisy. It wasn't home, but then he'd never really had a home, at least not one of his own. He'd lived with Max Henley a while, and that had seemed as close as he'd ever get to having a family. But that was before Max died. Ever since, his life had been centered on nailing Donner. Where he lived was a trivial matter.

He waited to see Emily's reactions to the apartment, but she didn't so much as blink. After a brief smile, she set the basket on the wobbly table, then opened it with a flourish. "Blueberry muffins, sausage links and fresh fruit." She flashed him a quick, sweet smile. "And coffee."

He was touched, he couldn't help it. "I can't believe you made me breakfast."

"It's not fancy, but you didn't strike me as a man who would want escargots so early in the morning."

He grimaced, then ended with a smile. "And you didn't strike me as the type who would cook for a man."

"I like to cook. My mother thinks it's some faulty gene inherited from my ancestors. But since I'm not married, I don't get to indulge very often."

"What about dates? You could do some real nice entertaining in your house."

She busied herself with setting out the food. "I don't go out much."

He wasn't immune to her vulnerability. He reached out and touched her hand. "No woman has ever cooked for me before."

She stared at him, shocked. "You're kidding."

Feeling a little stupid now for mentioning it, Judd shook his head. "Nope."

"What about your mother?"

"Left when I was real little. My father raised me."

"Oh." Then she tilted her head. "The two of you are close?"

He laughed. "Hardly. Dad stayed drunk most of the time, and I tried to stay out of his hair, 'cause Dad could get real mean when he drank."

"That's awful!" She looked so outraged on his behalf, he grinned.

"It wasn't as bad as all that, Em."

"Of course it was. I think it sounds horrid. Did you have any brothers or sisters?"

"Nope."

"So you were all alone?"

That was the softest, saddest voice he'd ever heard, and for some fool reason, he liked hearing it from her. "Naw. I had Max."

"Max?"

"Yeah. See, I wasn't all that respectable when I was younger, and Max Henley busted me trying to steal the tip he'd left for a waitress. With Max being a cop and all, I thought I'd end up in jail. But instead, he bought me lunch, chewed me out real good, then made me listen to about two hours' worth of lectures on right and wrong and being a good man. I was only fourteen, so I can't say I paid that much attention. When I finally got out of that restaurant, I didn't think I'd ever go back. But I did. See, I knew Max ate his lunch there every day, so the next day, when he saw me hanging around, he invited me to join him. It became a routine, and that summer, he gave me a job keeping up his yard. After a while, Max kind of became like family to me."

Emily was grinning now, too. "He was a father figure?"

"Father, mother, and sometimes as grumpy as an old schoolmarm. But he took good care of me. I guess you could say he was a complete 'family figure.'" *And Donner had robbed Judd of that family.*

"He sounds like a wonderful man."

"Yeah." Judd looked away, wishing he'd never brought up the subject. "Max was the best. He's dead now."

"I'm sorry."

Judd bit his upper lip, barely controlling the urge to hug her close. She had spoken so softly, with so much sincerity, her words felt like a caress. Somehow, she managed to lessen the pain he always felt whenever he thought of Max. God, he still missed him, though it had been nearly six months since Donner had killed him.

Judd nodded, then waited through an awkward silence while Emily looked around for something to do.

She went back to unloading her basket. As she opened the dishes, Judd inhaled the aromas. "Mmm. Smells good. Why don't you get things ready while I put on some pants. Okay?"

"I'll have the table set in a snap." Then she grinned again. "I hope you're hungry. I made plenty."

Judd shook his head. She was wooing him with breakfast, a ploy as old as mankind, and he was succumbing without a struggle. If he was ever going to keep her safe, he'd have to keep his head and maintain the control. The only way to do that was to make certain some distance existed between them. He couldn't be moved by every small gesture she made.

When he emerged from the bedroom two minutes later, Emily had everything on plates. He noticed there were two settings, so obviously she planned to eat with him. He also saw that, other than coffee mugs, she'd found only paper plates and plastic cutlery in his kitchen. But she didn't seem put off by that fact. A tall thermos of coffee sat in the middle of the table. It smelled strong, just the way he liked it.

"This is terrific, Emily. I appreciate it." Normally, he didn't eat breakfast, but his stomach growled as he approached the table, and he couldn't deny how hungry he was.

Emily poured his coffee, still smiling. "I thought we could talk while we eat. Maybe get to know each other a little better. I mean, we will be working together, and we're practically strangers."

He glanced up at her. "I wouldn't say that."

She blinked, then looked away. "How long have you been...ah..."

"Stripping?"

"Yes." There was another bright blush on her cheeks. Judd wondered how she kept from catching fire.

"A while," he said, keeping his answer vague.

"You...you like it?"

Good Lord. He laid down his fork and stared at her. She was the most unpredictable woman he'd ever met. Watching her eyes, he said, "Everyone should experience stripping at least once. It's a fantasy, but most people don't have the guts to try it."

She sucked in her breath. The fork she had in front of her held a piece of sausage, ready to fall off. She looked guilty.

Ah. He smiled, reading her thoughts. "Admit it, Emily. You've thought of it, haven't you? Imagine the men, or even one man, getting hotter with every piece of clothing you remove. Imagine his eyes staring at you, imagine him wanting you so bad he can't stand it. But you make him wait, until you're ready, until you're completely...naked."

She trembled, then put down her fork, folding her hands in her lap. Judd didn't feel like smiling now; he felt like laying her across the table, tossing the skirt of her dress up around her shoulders and viewing all of her, naked. For him. He wanted to drive into her slim body and hear her scream his name. It angered him, the unaccountable way she could provoke his emotions, leaving him raw.

"You want to strip for me, Emily? I'll be a willing audience, I can promise you that."

"Why are you doing this?"

Her tone was breathless, faint. With arousal or humiliation? He slashed his hand in the air, disgusted with himself. "Eat your breakfast."

"Judd..."

"I'm sorry, Emily. I'm not usually such a bastard. Just forget it, all right?"

She didn't look as though she wanted to. Instead, she looked ready to launch into another round of questions and he couldn't take it. He began eating, ignoring her, giving all his attention to his food.

He waited until she'd taken a bite of her muffin, then said, "I've decided if I'm going to help you, I'll need more information."

Emily swallowed quickly and looked at him, her eyes wide. "I told you everything."

"No. I need the whole truth now, Emily. How you're involved, and why. What really happened." He took a sip of coffee, watching her over the rim of his mug. "Who's the kid? But most of all, what does he have to do with you?"

4

EMILY KNEW her luck had just run out. And though it surprised her he'd figured her out so soon, she had expected it. Judd wasn't an idiot, far from it. And she supposed it was his obvious intelligence and insight that made her feel so sure he would help her.

How much to tell him was her quandary.

Judd evidently grew impatient with her silence. "Stop trying to think up some elaborate lie. You're no good at it, anyway. Hell, if I can tell you're planning to lie, you'll never be able to carry it off. So just the truth, if you please. Now."

Emily frowned at him. He didn't have to sound so surly. And he didn't have to look so...sexy. He'd shocked her but good, answering the door near-naked. Even now, with his pants on, he still looked sleep-rumpled and much too appealing. She cleared her throat and stared down at her plate.

"All I can tell you is that someone I hold dear was injured when that gun misfired. Since I know no one else is going to do anything about it, I have to. And the only thing I can think of is to make sure that the man who sold the gun is brought to justice."

"Is the guy a lover?"

Emily blinked. "Who?"

"The man who is *dear to you*."

His sneering tone had her leaning back in surprise. "Don't be ridiculous. He's just a boy. Only sixteen."

Judd shrugged. "So who is he? A relative?"

Why wouldn't he just let it rest? Why wouldn't he—

"*Dammit, Emily, who is he?*"

He shocked her so badly with his sudden shout, she blurted out, "My brother!"

"Ah. I suppose that could motivate a person. Never having had a brother myself, I wouldn't know for certain, of course. But I can see where you'd want to protect a little brother." Judd rubbed his whiskered jaw, then added, "Why don't your parents just go to the police?"

Emily stood up and walked away from the table. How had he gotten her to reveal so much, so easily? She knew she had no talent for subterfuge, but she hadn't thought she'd crack so quickly. When she turned to face Judd again, she caught him staring at her ankles. Her silence drew his attention, and when his gaze lifted to her face, he didn't apologize, but merely lifted a dark eyebrow.

Trying to ignore the heat in her face, Emily folded her hands over her waist and said, "My parents hate scandal more than anything. They'd rather move to another country than have their name sullied with damaging speculation."

"Don't they love their son?"

"Well, of course they do." Appalled that she'd given

him the wrong impression, Emily took her seat again, leaning forward to get his attention. "It's just that they've got some pretty strident notions about propriety. Their reputations, and the family name, mean a lot to them."

"More than their son, evidently." Then Judd shook his head. "No, Emily, don't start defending them again. I really don't give a damn what kind of parents you have. But it seems to me, if they're willing to sweep the incident under the carpet, you should be, too. What can you hope to prove, anyway?"

This was the tricky part, trying to make him understand how important it was for John to see now, before it was too late, exactly what road he was choosing. She didn't want to see the same disdain in Judd's eyes when she mentioned her brother as he apparently felt for her parents. Why his opinion mattered to her, she didn't know. But it did.

Keeping her voice low, she said, "John bought the gun, I think, because he wanted my parents' attention. You'd have to understand how hard he tried to find his...niche. I remember last Christmas, John was crushed when my parents sent him a gift from Europe." Her lips tilted in a vague smile. "It was a check, a substantial check, but still, it was only money. John sat in front of the stupid Christmas tree, seven feet high and professionally decorated, and he cried. I didn't let him know I was there because I knew it would embarrass him."

Judd looked down at his feet. "I never had a Christ-

mas tree until Max took me in. It was only a spindly little thing, but I liked it. It beat the hell out of seeing my
father passed out drunk in the front room where the
Christmas tree should have been but wasn't."

"Oh, Judd."

"Now, don't start, Em. We're talking about John, remember? I only mentioned that memory because I
guess I always assumed people with money had a better holiday. I mean, more gifts, better food, a lot of cheer
and all that." He shook his head. "Shoots that theory all
to hell, doesn't it?"

"People usually think having money is wonderful,
but that's not always true. Sometimes…money spoils
things. It can make people self-centered, maybe even
neglectful. Because it's so easy to do what you want,
when you want, it's easy to forget about the others
who…might depend on you. It's easy to forget that
everyone can't be bought, and money doesn't solve
every problem."

Judd didn't say a word, but his hand, so large and
warm and rough, curled around her fingers and held
on. Emily started, surprised at the gentleness of his
touch, at how comforting it felt to make physical contact
with him. She glanced up, and his eyes held hers. There
was no more derision, and certainly no pity. Only understanding.

It was nearly her undoing.

"My…my brother, he's a good kid, Judd, just a bit
misguided. And though he's trying to play it tough
right now, he's scared. He doesn't know if he'll ever

look the same as he did before the accident. My parents keep assuring him they'll find a good plastic surgeon to take care of everything, but he's hurting. Not physically, but inside. He wanted my parents' attention, but all he's gained is their annoyance. They never once asked him why he bought the gun or how. They only complained about him doing something so stupid. And they made it clear, had he wanted a gun, they could have bought the finest hunting rifle available, and supplied him with lessons on how to handle it."

"They missed the point entirely."

Emily felt his deep voice wash over her, and she smiled. "Yes, they did."

"Okay. So what will nailing the guy who sold him the gun prove to your brother?"

"That I love him. That I know what's right and wrong, and that he knows it, too, if he'll only open his eyes and realize that he is a good person, that he doesn't need affirmation from anyone but himself."

"Is that what you learned, honey? Do you understand your brother so well, because you've gone through the same thing?"

Emily forced a laugh and tried to pull her hand free, but Judd wouldn't let her go. He wouldn't let her look away, either. His gaze held her as securely as his fingers held her hand. "I've never felt the need to purchase a gun, Judd."

"No, but you must have wanted approval from your family as much as your brother does. What did you do, Emily, to get them to notice you?"

She cleared her throat and tried to change the subject. "This is ridiculous. It doesn't have anything to do with our deal."

"To hell with the deal. What did you do, Em?"

Panic began to edge through her. Not for anything would she lay the humiliation she'd suffered out for him to see. Besides, she'd buried the memory deep. It was no longer a part of her. At least, she hoped it wasn't.

"I've made my fair share of mistakes," she told him. "But I've forgiven myself and gotten on with my life. That's all any of us can do." Once she said that, she came to her feet, knowing she had to do something, occupy herself somehow, or she'd become maudlin. A display of emotions wouldn't serve her purpose.

But as she stood, so did Judd, and before she could move away, he had her tugged close. The morning whiskers on his jaw felt slightly abrasive, and arousing, as he brushed against her cheek. The warmth of his palms seeped through her dress to her back where he carefully stroked her in a comforting, soothing manner. She could smell his musky, male scent, and breathed deeply, filling herself with him, uncaring what had brought on this show of concern. It simply felt too good to have him hold her.

"You should always remember, Em, what a good person you are. Don't let anyone convince you otherwise."

His raspy tone sounded close to her ear, sending gooseflesh up her arms. And her emotions must have been closer to the surface than she'd wanted to admit, because she could feel the sting of tears behind her lids.

Not wanting Judd to know how he affected her, she hid her face in his shoulder and tried a laugh. It sounded a little wobbly, but it was the best she could produce. "You hardly know me, Judd. What makes you think I'm such a fine specimen of humanity?"

He rocked her from side to side, and she could hear the smile in his voice when he spoke. "Are you kidding me? You're obviously damn loyal since you're willing to risk your pretty little neck for your brother, just to keep him on the right track. You've opened your property to the neighborhood kids, not caring that they might trample your flowers or muddy up your yard. And you told me you volunteer at the soup kitchen. I'll bet you've got a whole group of charity organizations you donate to, don't you?"

Emily squeezed herself closer, loving the solid feel of his chest against her cheek, the strength of his arms around her. She couldn't recall ever feeling so safe. "I'm the one who benefits from the organizations. I've met so many really good, caring people, who just need a little help to get their lives straightened out. We talk, we laugh. Sometimes...I don't know what I'd do without them."

Judd groaned, and then his hand was beneath her chin, tilting her face up. Emily smiled, thinking he had a few more questions for her, when his mouth closed over hers and she couldn't think at all.

Heat was her first impression. The added warmth

seemed to be everything, touching her everywhere. She felt it in her toes as he lifted her to meet him better, to fit her more fully against him. She felt it in her breasts, pressed tight against his chest. And in her stomach, as the heat curled and expanded.

His mouth was firm, his tongue wet as he licked over her lips, insisting she open. When she did, he tasted her deeply, his hands coming up to hold her face still as he slanted his mouth over hers again and again.

Emily had never known such a kiss. She'd thought she'd experienced lust while she was engaged, but it had been nothing like this. She made a small sound of surprise, wanting the contact to go on forever—and suddenly Judd pulled away.

Emily grabbed the back of the chair to keep herself grounded. Judd stared at her, looking appalled and fascinated and...hungry. *Oh, Lord, Emily, now you've really done it.*

She should have felt guilty for behaving so improperly, but all her mind kept repeating was, *Let's do it again.* She shook her head at herself, dismissing that errant notion and trying to remember her purpose. Judd must have misunderstood, because he turned away.

"I'm sorry," he said.

Emily blinked several times. "I beg your pardon?"

Judd whirled to face her, once again furious. "I said, I'm sorry, dammit. I shouldn't have done that. It won't happen again."

Oh, darn. "No, of course not. It was my fault. I

shouldn't have been telling you all my problems and—"

"Shut up, Emily."

She did, and stared at him, waiting to see what he would do, what he wanted her to do.

"Damn." He snatched her close again, pressed another hard, entirely too quick kiss to her lips, then set her away. "I take it back. It probably will happen again. Hopefully, not for a while, but...I'm not making any promises. If you don't want me ever to touch you, just say so, all right?"

Emily remained perfectly still, unwilling to take a chance that he might misunderstand her response if she moved. She prided herself on the fact she wasn't a hypocrite. No, she wanted Judd, and she was thrilled beyond reason that he apparently wanted her, too. And since he held rather obvious scorn for her background—that of money and privilege—he wouldn't expect her to play the part of the proper lady. No, Judd had already made it clear where his preferences lay. Any man who could strip for a living was obviously on the earthy side, primal and lusty and...her heart skipped two beats while she waited to see what he'd do next.

He laughed. It wasn't a humorous laugh, but one of wonder and disbelief. "You're something else, Emily, you know that? Here, sit down." He loosened her death grip on the chair back and nudged her toward the seat. "Don't go away. I'm going to shower and finish getting dressed, then we'll make some plans, okay?"

She sat. She nodded. She felt ready to explode with anticipation.

Judd ruffled her hair, still shaking his head, and left the room.

HE MADE CERTAIN it was a cold shower, but the temperature of the water didn't help to cool the heat of his body. Never could he remember being hit so hard. Holding her felt right, talking to her felt right. Hell, kissing her had been as right as it could get—bordering on blissful death.

He could only imagine how it would feel to...no. He'd better not imagine or he'd find himself right back in the shower.

How could one woman be so damn sweet? He'd have thought all that money and her parents' attitudes would have soured her, but it hadn't. Emily loved. She loved her brother, she loved the children in her neighborhood. She even loved the homeless who visited the kitchen where she volunteered. He'd heard it in her tone, seen it in her eyes.

God, she was killing him.

He had to stay objective, and that meant getting back to business. He finished dragging a comb through his damp hair and left the bathroom.

Emily hadn't moved a single inch. And if he hadn't already had a little taste of her, he'd believe her prissy pose, with her knees pressed tightly together, and her slim hands folded in her lap. Ha! What a facade. He dragged his eyes away from her wary gaze and began stuffing her thermos and empty dishes back into the basket. "You ready to go?"

"Ah...go where?"

He flicked an impatient glance her way. "To find your gun dealer. I thought we'd hit some of the local establishments. The pool hall, first. Then maybe the diner. And tonight, the bar."

"Are you...dancing tonight?"

"No. I've got all weekend free. I only dance on Tuesdays and Thursdays, remember?" He noticed her sigh of relief and frowned at her. "But you will be there when I dance, Em. To pull this off, you're going to have to be my biggest fan. Everyone will have to believe I'm yours. You can be as territorial as you like. Besides, I can use you as a smoke screen. If the ladies all believe I'm already spoken for, they might not be so persistent."

Emily pursed her lips, her shoulders going a little straighter. "Are you certain that's what you want? I don't wish to interfere in your social life."

"You know, Em, you don't sound the least bit sincere."

She looked totally flustered now, and it was all he could do not to laugh. "Come on, let's get going."

Holding her arm, a manner that felt as right as everything else he did with her, Judd hustled her down to the street and into his truck. He waited until she'd settled herself, then asked, "Did your brother mention what the guy who sold him the gun looked like?"

Emily shook her head. "He wasn't in much condition

to talk when I saw him last. I did get him to tell me where he'd bought it, though. But all he said about the man was that he'd grinned when he sold him the gun."

Judd noticed she'd tucked her hands into fists again, and he reached over to entwine her fingers with his. "When was your brother hurt?"

"Not quite a month ago. I saw him right afterward and then my parents took him away as soon as the hospital allowed it. I didn't even get to say goodbye."

"So you have no idea how he's doing?"

Emily turned away to stare out the side window. Her voice dropped to a low pitch, indicating her worry. "I've talked to him on the phone. He...he's very depressed. Though my parents evidently refuse to believe it, the plastic surgeons have already done all they can. The worst of the scars have been minimized. But the burns from the backfire did some extensive damage to the underlying tissue around his upper cheek and temple. He claims his face still looks horrid, but I don't believe it's as bad as he thinks. He's...he's always been popular in school, especially with the girls. I guess he thinks his life is over. I tried to make him look on the positive side, that his eyesight wasn't permanently damaged, but I don't suppose he can see a bright side right now."

Her voice broke, but Judd pretended he hadn't heard. He instinctively knew she wouldn't appreciate her loss of control. For such a small woman, she had an overabundance of pride and gumption, and he had no intention of denting it.

He squeezed her fingers again and kept his eyes focused on the road. "When will he be home again?"

"I don't know. I haven't spoken with my parents." She sent him a tilted smile. "They're blaming me for this. They say I'm a bad influence on him."

"You?" Judd couldn't hide his surprise.

"I work with the underprivileged. I don't own a single fur coat. And I live in an old house that constantly needs repair."

"Your house? I thought your house was terrific."

She seemed genuinely pleased by his praise. "Thank you. But the plumbing is dreadful. I've had almost everything replaced, but now the hot-water heater is about to go. Either the water is ice-cold, or so hot it could scald you. I thought my father would disown me when he burned his hand on the kitchen faucet. But even more than my house, my parents hate that I refuse to marry a man they approve of. They want me to 'settle into my station in life.'" Emily laughed. "Doesn't that sound ridiculous?"

"Settling down? Not really. I think you'd make a fantastic wife and mother." Dead silence followed his claim, and Judd could have bitten his tongue in two. It was bad enough that he still yearned for a real family. But to say as much to Emily? She was probably worried, especially after that kiss he'd given her, that he might have designs on her.

He slanted a look her way, and noticed a bright blush on her cheeks. Trying to put her at ease, he said, "You look like a domestic little creature, Em. That's all I meant."

Those wide brown eyes of hers blinked, and then she started mumbling to herself. He couldn't quite catch what she was saying. Judging from the tone, though, he probably wouldn't want to hear it, anyway. He had the suspicion she was giving him a proper set-down—in her own, polite way.

Judd was contemplating her reaction, and the reason for it, when they pulled up in front of the pool hall. It was still early, well before noon, so he didn't expect the place to be overly crowded. Only the regulars would be there, the men who made shooting pool an active part of their livelihood.

Clayton Donner was one of those men.

Judd didn't expect to see him here today, but he never knew when he might get lucky. And in the meantime, he'd find out a little more about Donner.

Emily was silent as he led her into the smoky interior. Unlike the lighting at the bar, it was bright here, and country music twanged from a jukebox in the far corner. Some of the men looked as if they'd been there all night and the low-hanging fluorescent lights added a gray cast to their skin. Others looked merely bored, and still others were intent on their game. But they all looked up at Emily. Judd could feel her uneasiness, but for the moment, he played his role and, other than put his arm around her shoulders to mark his claim, he payed her little attention.

Leaning down to whisper in her ear, he said, "Play

along with me now. And remember, no matter what happens, don't lose your cool." Then he gave her a kiss on the cheek and a swat on the behind. "Get me a drink, will ya, honey?"

He gave a silent prayer she'd do as she was told, then sauntered over to the nearest table. "Hey, Frog. You been here all night?"

Frog, as his friends called him, had a croak for a voice, due to a chop to the larynx that had damaged his throat during a street fight. Frog didn't croak now, though. He was too busy watching Emily as she made her way cautiously to the bar, careful not to touch anyone or anything.

Judd gave a feral grin. "That's mine, Frog, so put your eyes back in your head."

Frog grunted. "What the hell are you doing with her? She ain't your type."

Judd shrugged. "She's rich. She's my type."

Frog thought that was hilarious, and was still laughing when Emily carried a glass of cola to Judd. He took a sip, then choked. Glaring in mock anger, Judd demanded, "What the hell is that?"

Emily raised her eyebrows, but didn't look particularly intimidated by his tone. "A drink?"

"Damn, I don't want soda. I meant a real drink." Actually, Judd never touched liquor. He knew alcoholism tended to run in families, and after living with his father, he wouldn't ever take the chance of becoming like him. Still, he handed the glass back to Emily, then said with disgust, "You drink it. And stay out of my way. I'm going to shoot some pool here with Frog."

Emily huffed. She started to walk away, but Judd caught her arm and she landed against his chest. Before she could draw a breath, he kissed her. It wasn't a killer kiss like the one he'd given her earlier, but it was enough to show everyone they were definitely an item. He drew away, but couldn't resist giving her a quick, soft peck before adding, "Behave yourself, honey. I won't be long."

Emily nodded, apparently appeased, and went to perch on a stool. Judd looked at her a moment longer, appreciating the pretty picture she made, waiting there for him. She dutifully smiled, and looked as if she'd wait all day if that was what he wanted.

It was the kind of fantasy he could really get into, having a woman like Emily for his own. But he couldn't spare the time or the energy to get involved with her or anyone else. He needed, and wanted, to focus all his attention on taking Donner off the streets. The man had stolen a huge hunk of his life when he'd killed Max. Judd wasn't ever going to forget that.

So instead of indulging in the pleasure he got by simply watching Emily, he turned away. He knew she didn't realize what he'd done, making her look like a woman he could control with just a little physical contact, but every man in the room understood.

And even though that had been his intent, Judd hated every damn one of them for thinking that about Emily. It was bad enough that he'd sold himself to trap Donner, but now he was selling Emily, too. It didn't sit right with him, but at the moment, his choices were limited, and the only alternative was to postpone his plans. Which was really no alternative at all.

EMILY HAD NO IDEA investigating could be so exhausting, though Judd did the actual work. All she did was pretend to be his ornament. It rankled, but until she could get him alone and set him straight about how this little partnership was going to work, she didn't want to take the chance of messing things up.

Judd had been shooting pool for quite some time when the door opened and three men walked in. One was a heavyset man, dirty and dressed all in black, with the name Jonesie written across his T-shirt. Another was a relatively young man, looking somewhat awed by his own presence.

It was the third man, though, that caught and held Emily's attention. There was something about him, a sense of self-confidence, that set him apart. He didn't look like a criminal, but something about him made Emily uncomfortable. He wore only a pair of pleated slacks and a polo shirt. His blond ponytail was interesting, but not actually unusual. In truth, Emily supposed he could be called handsome, but he held no appeal for her. He simply seemed too...pompous.

When his gaze landed on her, she quickly looked away and kept her eyes focused on Judd. And because she was watching Judd so intently, she saw the almost imperceptible stiffening of his body. He'd only glanced up once to see who had walked in, then he'd continued with his shot, smoothly pocketing the nine ball. But Emily felt she was coming to know him well enough to see the tension in his body.

She was still pondering the meaning of that tension when the men approached where she sat.

"Hey, Clay, you want something to drink?"

The blonde smiled toward Emily and took the stool next to her before answering Jonesie. "No. I'm fine. I think I'll just watch the...scenery, for a while."

Emily wanted to move away, but she didn't. Not even on the threat of death would she turn and meet that smile, though she felt it as the man, Clay, continued to watch her. When he touched her arm, she jumped.

"Well, now, honey. No need to be nervous. I was only going to get acquainted."

Emily shook her head and tried to shrug his hand away. Instead of complying with her obvious wish, his well-manicured fingers curled around her arm. His touch repulsed her. She jumped off the stool and stepped back...right into the younger of the three men. She was caught.

This was nothing like talking to the drunks the other night. She'd felt some sense of control then. But now, as Clay chuckled at her reaction and reached out to stroke her cheek, she felt a scream catch in her throat. His fingers almost touched her skin—and then Judd was there, gripping the man's arm by the wrist and looking as impenetrable as a stone wall.

"The lady is mine. And no one touches her but me."

JUDD NARROWED his eyes, hoping, without the benefit of common sense, that Clayton would take him up on his challenge. He knew he wasn't thinking straight. He could destroy his entire case if he unleashed his temper now, but at the moment, none of that mattered.

He'd kept Donner in his sights from the moment he'd walked in, and he'd thought he'd be able to keep his cool even after Donner noticed Emily. But he hadn't counted on Emily's reaction.

When he'd seen her face and realized she was frightened, all he'd cared about was getting to her, staking his claim and making certain she knew there was nothing to fear. The fact that she was afraid should have angered him, and probably would once he had time to think about it. Didn't she know he wouldn't let anyone hurt her? Hell, he'd take the whole place apart before he'd see her hair get mussed.

But he supposed she couldn't know that, because even now, with him beside her, she still looked horrified. And then she got a hold of herself and smiled, a false smile, to be sure, and stepped to his side. "It's okay, Judd. Really."

Clayton looked down at his wrist where Judd still held him. The gesture was a silent command to be released, but Judd wasn't exactly in an accommodating mood. He tightened his hold for the briefest of seconds, gaining a raised eyebrow from Donner, then he let go. The younger man took a step forward, and Judd bared his teeth in a parody of a grin, encouraging him.

Emily seemed nearly frantic now, saying, "Come on, Judd. Let's go."

But he had no intention of going anywhere. Emily didn't know, couldn't know, the riot of emotions he was suffering right now. His desire to avenge Max mixed with his need to protect Emily, and he felt ready to explode with repressed energy. This was what he'd been waiting for. He could feel Donner's interest, his curiosity, and he knew he'd finally succeeded. If Donner's crony wanted to take him on, he was ready. More than ready. At this point, Donner would only be impressed with his ruthlessness. His muscles twitched in anticipation.

Then Donner laughed. "Don't be a fool, Mick. Our friend here is only trying to protect his interests. I can understand that."

The young man, Mick, moved away, but he did so reluctantly. Judd flexed his hands and tried to get himself under control. He stared at Clayton, then nodded and turned away, making certain he blocked Emily with his body. He knew Donner wouldn't like being dismissed, but he also didn't want to appear too eager.

Frog was standing at the pool table with his mouth hanging open, and Judd had to remind him it was his shot.

"No more for me," Frog said. "I'm done."

And in the next instant, Clayton was there, slapping Frog on the back and smiling. "So, what do you have for me, Frog?"

Frog pulled money out of his pocket, looking decidedly uncomfortable, and handed the bills to Clayton. As he counted, Clayton continued to smile, and then he asked, "That's it?"

Frog shifted his feet, glancing up at Judd and then away again. "I lost some of it."

"Is that so?"

Judd carefully laid his pool cue on the table then faced Clayton with a smile. He couldn't have asked for a better setup. "It seems I was having a lucky morning." His smile turned deliberately mocking, and he flicked his own stack of bills.

Again, Mick started forward, clearly unwilling to overlook such an insult to Clayton, and this time Jonesie was with him. But again, Clayton raised a hand. "Let's not be hasty." And to Judd, he said, "I'd like to meet the man who just took two hundred dollars of my money."

Judd heard Emily gasp, but he ignored her surprise. "Your money? Now, how can that be, when Frog told me he'd won that money last night shooting pool? And now that I've won it, I'd say it's my money."

Clayton lost his smile. "Do I know you from somewhere?"

Mick blurted out, "He's one of them strippers. I seen him at the bar the other night."

"Ah, that's right. I remember now. You've been something of a sensation, haven't you?"

Judd shrugged. "Hey, I make a buck wherever I can. A man can't be overly choosy."

"Obviously." Clayton looked down a moment, then his smile reappeared. "Maybe we can do business together sometime. I have several different ventures that might interest you. Especially since you're not choosy."

Again, Judd shrugged, careful not to show his savage satisfaction. Then he took Emily by the arm. "Maybe." He deliberately dismissed Clayton once more, knowing it would infuriate him, but probably intrigue him, as well. As he started out the door, he said, "You can look me up if anything really...interesting comes along."

They were barely out the door, when Emily started to speak. Judd squeezed her arm. "Not a word, Em. Not one single word."

The tension was still rushing through him, and he knew Clayton was watching them through the large front glass of the pool hall. Playing it cool had never been so difficult; no other assignment had been so personal. Playing up to Donner turned his stomach and filled him with rage. He wanted to hit something. He wanted to shout.

He wanted to make love to Emily.

But, he couldn't do any of those things, so he had to content himself with the knowledge he'd set Clayton up good. Not only had he more or less managed to steal two hundred dollars Clayton had earmarked as his own, but he knew damn well Clayton didn't consider their business finished. Not by a long shot. He'd hear from Donner again, and soon.

He only hoped he could manage to keep Emily out of the way.

5

EMILY THOUGHT she'd shown great restraint and a good deal of patience. But her patience was now at an end.

Judd had refused to talk to her while he aimlessly drove around the lower east side, burning off his sour mood and occasionally grunting at the questions she asked. Twice they had stopped while he got out of the truck and talked to different people loitering on the sidewalk. Emily had been instructed to wait in the pickup.

When she asked him what he was doing, he'd said only, "Investigating." When she asked what he'd found out, he'd said, "Quiet. Let me think."

It had been nearly two hours since they'd left the pool hall, and her frustration had grown with each passing minute. She tried to maintain her decorum, tried to keep her temper in check and behave in a civilized manner, but he was making that impossible. *You're the boss here, Emily. You hired him. Demand a few answers.* She decided she would do exactly that, when Judd pulled up in front of the diner.

Apparently, he expected her to get out and follow him like a well-trained puppy, because he stepped out and started to walk away without a single word to her. She refused to budge.

Of course, Judd was halfway through the diner door before he realized she was still in the truck. Then he did an about-face, and stomped back to her side, looking very put out. "What's the holdup?"

Emily gave him a serene smile. "I want to talk to you."

"So? Let's get a seat inside and you can talk. God knows, that's all you've done for the past hour, anyway."

She stiffened with the insult, but refused to lower herself to his irritating level. "You're not going to make me angry, Judd. I know you're just trying to get me off the track. But I want to know what that was all about in the pool hall. And don't you dare shake your head at me again!"

He looked undecided for a long moment, then let out a disgusted sigh. "All right, all right. Come in, sit, and we'll...talk."

Emily wasn't certain she believed him, he still looked as stubborn as a mule, but she left the truck and allowed Judd to lead her inside. They sat at a back booth, and a waitress immediately came to take their order. The woman seemed a little hostile to Emily, then she all but melted over Judd.

Judd treated her to a full smile and a wink. "You got anything for me, Suze?"

You got anything for me, Suze, Emily silently repeated, thinking Suze had just received a much warmer greeting from Judd than she herself had managed to garner all day.

The waitress looked over at Emily, one slim eyebrow lifted, and Judd grinned. "She's fine. Just tell me what you've got."

"Well..."

Emily rolled her eyes. Suze obviously had a flair for the dramatic, given the way she glanced around the diner in a covert manner, as if she were preparing to part with government secrets. She also patted her platinum blond hair and primped for a good ten seconds before finally exalting them with her supposed wisdom. *What a waste of time.*

Emily no sooner had that thought than she regretted it. Suze turned out to be a fount of information.

"He's been in twice since we spoke and something is definitely going down. He met with the same guy both times, that punk kid who distributes for him. I'd say something will happen within a week or two. That's usually the routine, you know."

"You couldn't catch an actual date?"

"Hell, no, sugar. If Donner caught me snooping, he'd have my fanny."

Judd reached out to smack the fanny-in-peril. "We wouldn't want that to happen. But Suze? If anything more concrete comes up, you know where to find me."

She knew where to find him? Emily knew she had no right to be jealous. After all, her relationship with Judd was strictly business. But still, she didn't like the idea of him...consorting with this woman. Of course, Suze seemed to know a great deal about the gun dealer. In fact, she seemed to know almost too much. Emily narrowed her eyes, wondering exactly when Judd had contacted this woman, and what their relationship might be. Judd seemed to be on awfully familiar terms with her.

But Suze did appear to be helping, and Emily certainly had no claims on Judd. She decided to concentrate on that fact, but she couldn't keep herself from glaring at the waitress. Suze didn't seem to notice.

She was back to primping. "Of course I know where you'll be. I wouldn't miss an act. Do something special for me Tuesday night, all right?"

Judd laughed and shook his head.

Suddenly, Suze was all-business. "You two want anything to drink or something? It don't look right me standing here gabbing without you orderin' anything."

"Two coffees, Suze. That's it."

Emily barely waited for the waitress to go swaying away before she leaned across the table and demanded Judd's attention. "Was she talking about who I think she was talking about?"

"Who did you think she was—"

"That's not funny, Judd!"

"No, I guess it isn't. And yes, she was talking about our friendly, neighborhood gun trafficker."

Emily was aghast. "She *knows* him?" She couldn't believe the waitress had called him by name. Why, if he was that well known...

"Everyone knows who commits the crimes, Em. It's just coming up with proof that's so damn difficult."

Her breath caught in her throat and she choked. "You know who he is, too?"

Judd shrugged, his eyes dropping to the top of the table. Then he quirked a sardonic smile. "You met him yourself, honey."

"I did..." Suddenly it fit, and Emily fell back against the seat. "The guy at the pool hall?"

"Yep. That was him. Clayton Donner."

It took her a minute, and then she felt the steam. It had to be coming out her ears, she was so enraged. Judd had let her get close to the man who'd hurt her brother, and he hadn't even told her.

He was speaking to her now, but she couldn't hear him over the ringing in her ears. Her entire body felt taut, and her stomach felt queasy. No wonder she had reacted so strongly to that man. He'd been that close and...

Emily didn't make a conscious decision on what to do. She just suddenly found herself standing then walking toward the door. She somehow knew Judd was following, though she didn't turn to look. When she stepped outside, and started past his truck, he grabbed her arm and pulled her around to face him.

"Dammit, Emily! What the hell is the matter with you?"

"Let me go." She felt proud of the strength in her voice, though she knew she might fall apart at any moment.

"Are you kidding? I've tried every damn intimidation tactic I could think of—"

"Ha! So you admit to bullying me?"

"—to send you running, but you clung like flypaper. And now, with one little scare, you want me to turn you loose?"

Flypaper! How dare he compare her to... No, Emily, don't get sidetracked by a measly insult. The man deceived you. She lifted her chin and met his gaze. "I wish to leave now. Alone."

"No way, baby. You wanted in, and now you're in."

Her heartbeat shook her, it pounded so hard, and her fingers ached from being held in such tight fists. If she wasn't a lady, she'd smack him one, but good. "When were you going to tell me, Judd? When?"

Judd stiffened, and his jaw went hard. "Get in the truck, Em."

"I will not. I..."

"Get in the damn truck!"

Well. Put that way... Emily became aware of people watching, and also that Judd was every bit as angry as she was. But why? What possible reason did he have for being so mad? She was the one who'd been misled, kept in the dark, lied to...well, not really. But lies of omission definitely counted, and Judd had omitted telling her a great deal.

And after he'd insisted she bare her soul.

When he continued to glare at her, she realized how foolish they both must appear, and she opened the truck door to get in. It wouldn't do to make a public spectacle of herself.

"Put your seat belt on."

Emily stared out her window, determined not to answer him, to ignore him as completely as he'd ignored her all day. But then she muttered, *"Flypaper."*

She heard Judd make a small sound that could have been a chuckle but she didn't look to see. If the man dared to smile, she'd probably forget all about avoiding a scene. But then, thoughts of attacking that gorgeous body left her a little breathless, and she decided ignoring him was better, by far.

Judd reached over and strapped her in. He stayed leaning close for a second or two, then flicked his finger over her bottom lip. "Stop pouting, Em, and act like an adult."

It took a major effort, but she didn't bite that finger. She could just imagine how appalled her parents would have been by that thought.

Judd's sigh was long and drawn-out. "Fine. Have it your way, honey. But if you decide you want to talk, just speak up."

Fifteen minutes later, Emily was wishing she could do just that. Judd pulled into her driveway with the obvious intent of being well rid of her, and she desperately didn't want him to go. She felt confused and still angry and...hurt. If he could explain, then maybe she could forgive him and... *And what, Emily? Maybe he'd let you have one of those killer smiles like the one he gave Suze?* She'd been taken in by one man, and though she honestly believed Judd was different, she wouldn't, couldn't, put all her trust in him. Not on blind faith. Not without some explanations.

When all was said and done, he worked for her, and she deserved to know what was going on. She had to find evidence against Donner, and she needed Judd to do that. But only if he didn't shut her out.

He stopped the truck, and she sat there, trying to think of some way, without losing every ounce of pride, to talk things out with him.

But Judd saved her the trouble. He got out of the pickup, slamming his door then stomping over to the passenger side. She stared at him, her eyes wide with surprise, when he opened the door and hauled her out.

"What do you think you're doing?" His hold was gentle on her arm as he led her up the steps to her back door. She practically had to run to keep up with his long-legged, impatient stride.

"We're going to talk, Em. I don't like you treating me as if I've just kicked your puppy."

Uh-oh. He sounded even angrier than she'd first assumed. "I don't even have a dog—"

Judd snatched her key from her hand, unlocked the door and ushered her inside. "Do you need to punch in your code for the alarm system?"

It took her a second to comprehend his words since her mind still wrestled with why he was in her house, and what he planned to do there. "Oh, ah, no. I only turn it on when I'm in the house. The rest of the time, I just lock up."

Judd stared. "Why the hell would you get a fancy alarm system, and not use it?"

"Because twice I forgot to turn it off when I came in, and the outside alarms went off, and then several neighbors showed up at my door and the central office called, and it was embarrassing." Judd rolled his eyes in exasperation, and Emily felt her cheeks heat. She hadn't meant to tell him all that. "Judd? I don't want to talk about my alarm system."

Looking restless and still a bit angry, Judd paced across the kitchen. Then he stalked back to her. "Tell me this, Emily. What would you have done if I'd spoken up and introduced you to Donner?"

She watched as he propped his hands on his hips and glared at her. "I don't know what I would have done. But I know I would have done...something."

"Something like accuse him? Or something like demand he give himself up? I thought you needed proof? I thought that was what we were doing, trying to nail him."

His scowl was much more fierce than her own, and her anger diminished to mere exasperation. The man could be so remarkably impossible. "We?" she asked, lacing her tone with sarcasm. "There was certainly no 'we' today. You've refused to tell me anything." When he crossed his arms, looking determined, she added in a gentler tone, "Judd, I can't very well find evidence against this Donner person if I don't know who he is."

Judd came to stand in front of her and gripped her shoulders. "I was working on finding evidence. Or did you think I just enjoyed toying with that bastard? Besides, you were scared out of your wits, Em. And that was without knowing who he was. He had a damn strange effect on you, which now that I think of it again, isn't very complimentary for me. I thought you knew I wouldn't let anyone hurt you."

Emily swallowed, feeling a tinge of guilt. "I'm sorry. Of course I assume you'll protect me, but—"

"Don't assume, Emily. Know. As long as you do as I tell you and follow my lead, you won't get hurt."

"Just like that? You tell me what to do, and I do it, no questions asked? I'm not a child, Judd—"

"So I noticed."

"And... You noticed?" Emily quickly shook her head so she wouldn't get sidetracked. "If you want me to trust you, you have to be totally honest with me, not just expect me to sit around and watch you work, without telling me what you're working on."

"You're making too much of this. I was only shooting pool."

"But you had a goal in mind. And you kept that from me. I despise dishonesty, Judd. I won't tolerate it." He winced, but she didn't give him time to interrupt. "I had no idea today that you were deliberately taking money from one of Donner's men. If I had known, maybe I wouldn't have been so surprised..."

"Exactly. Do you think I want Donner or any other punk to look at you and think you know the score?"

That silenced Emily for a moment. Why would Judd

care what other men thought of her? "I quit worrying about others' opinions long ago."

"Why?"

"What do you mean, 'why'?"

"Everyone cares what other people think, even when they know it shouldn't matter."

Busying her fingers by pleating and unpleating her skirt, Emily felt her exasperation grow. "Certain things...happened in my past, that assured me public opinion meant very little, but that honesty meant a great deal."

"Like what?"

When she didn't answer, he said, "Okay, we'll come back to that later."

"No, we won't."

"Dammit, Em. I'd much rather you come off looking like an innocent out for a few kicks, than to have some jerk assume you've been around."

Emily swallowed hard. Judd had evidently made some incorrect assumptions about her character, and it was up to her to explain the truth. "Judd, I don't know why you persist in thinking I'm...I'm innocent. I believe I told you once that I'd been engaged. Well..."

She couldn't look at him, her eyes were locked on her busy fingers. And then she heard him chuckle. Her gaze shot to his face, and she was treated to the most tender smile she'd ever seen.

"Honey, it wouldn't matter if you'd been engaged twenty times. You're still so damn innocent, you terrify me."

Emily didn't understand that statement, or the way he reached out and touched her cheek, then smoothed her hair behind her ear.

She felt disoriented, and much too warm. She wanted to lean into Judd, but she knew she had to settle things before she forgot what it was that she wanted settled. Once before she'd let her passionate nature guide her. That had been a huge error, and this was too important to be sidetracked by anything—including Judd's heated effect on her.

"The thing is, Em, this whole deal will work out better if your reactions to Donner and his men are real. You can't lie worth a damn, and I don't think, if Donner got close again, you'd be able to hide your feelings from him. You could blow everything."

She cleared her throat and spoke with more conviction than she actually felt. "You don't know that for sure."

His expression hardened, turning grim. "And I'm not willing to take the risk. Things could backfire real easy, and someone could get hurt."

She understood his reasoning, but she couldn't accept it. "This isn't going to work, Judd. Not unless you're willing to tell me everything."

He stared at her, hard, then muttered a curse and looked away. "No, you're right. It won't work. Which is why I've come up with an alternate plan. I decided I'd just find this guy for you, but on my own. You can stay in your little palace and play it safe."

"*What?*"

"You heard me. From here on, you're out of it."

Emily sputtered, then stiffened her spine. "You said I was 'in,' remember?"

"I've changed my mind."

"Well, you can just unchange it, because I'm not going to be left out."

"I refuse to risk your getting hurt, and your reaction today was proof positive you aren't ready to mingle with the meaner side of life. Let's face it, Em, you're just a baby."

"Oh, no, you don't." She propped her hands on her hips and glared at him. "You're not going to pull me into an argument by slinging horrid insults at me. We had a deal and you're the one who isn't following the rules. Well, you can just stop it right now."

He blinked at her in amazement. "I wasn't insulting you, dammit!"

Emily could tell by his expression he hadn't seen anything insulting in his attitude. But that only made the insult worse. She pursed her lips and tilted her head back so she could look down her nose at him. "I'm not entirely helpless, Judd. I can take care of myself."

There was a minute curving of his lips before he shook his head and spoke in a gentle, but firm, tone. "I'm sorry, Em. My mind's made up."

He acted as if he hadn't just dumped her, as if he hadn't just let her down and destroyed all her plans. But it was even more than her plans now. It was Judd, and she cared about him. She took one step closer and poked him in the chest with her finger. "Okay, fine. You don't want to help me, then I'll find another way."

Startled, he grabbed her finger and held on. "You already have a way. Me. I can do this, you know. I'm more than capable, and I damn sure don't need you looking after me. It'll be easier without you."

That hurt, but she didn't show it. She lifted her chin and met his intent gaze. "No. I won't let you risk yourself for me, not while I sit around and do nothing."

Judd bit his upper lip and his eyes narrowed. He suddenly looked...dangerous, and Emily shivered in expectation of what he might say. She knew it would be something outrageous, but she was prepared for the worst.

"So you'll pay me a five-hundred-dollar bonus. No big deal."

He had a very credible sneer. Emily frowned. She couldn't believe he'd just said that. And she couldn't believe he was really doing this only for the money. She couldn't have been that wrong.

A deep breath didn't help to relieve the sudden pain in her chest, or the tightness in her throat. She still sounded strained as she whispered, "Fine, if money's the issue, I'll pay you to forget you ever met me." She waited for his reaction, and though Judd remained rigid, she noticed his hands were now curled into tight fists.

There's a reaction for you, Emily. He doesn't seem at all pleased by being bought off. She decided to push him, just to see what it would take to force him to drop his charade. "Five thousand dollars, Judd. But I don't want you risking yourself. Take it or leave it." Then she opened the door and waited to see if he would actually leave.

"Damn you, Emily." The door slammed shut and she found herself pinned to the wall by his hard chest, his arms caging her in, his lips pressed to her hair. She could hear him panting, struggling for control of his temper.

Relief washed over her—and hot excitement. "Judd?"

He didn't answer. He kissed her instead, and if the first kiss had been hungry, this one was ravenous. Emily moaned and wrapped her arms around him, holding him tight as his tongue pushed deep into her mouth. How she'd come to care so much about him so quickly, she didn't know. Perhaps it was because she sensed the same emptiness in him that she'd often felt. When he'd told of his past, as different as it was from hers, she still saw a lot of similarities.

Emily knew she was being fanciful, but she couldn't deny the way she felt. It seemed to her sometimes there were no real heroes left in the world, people willing to do what was right—just because it was the right thing to do.

But Judd was a hero, despite his chosen profession, despite his lack of manners and sometimes overbearing arrogance. A hero was a man who could do what needed to be done, when it was needed. And Judd was as capable as they came.

"Oh, Em." His mouth touched her throat, her chin, then her lips again. "I have to stop."

She tried to shake her head, since stopping was the last thing she wanted, but she couldn't. His hands cupped her cheeks and he had her pressed flush against the wall, pinned from chest to knees, his erection hard and throbbing against her belly. It was glorious. She was well and truly trapped, and she loved it. "Judd..."

"No, honey." He was still breathing hard, his mouth touching soft and warm against her flesh, planting small biting kisses that tingled and tickled and stole her breath. "Neither one of us is ready for this. Hell, you've got me so crazy, I don't know what I'm doing. I need time to think. And so do you."

Don't beg, Emily. Don't beg. "Judd...I—"

He touched her lips with his thumb, then his eyes dropped to where she knew her nipples puckered tight against the front of her dress. His voice, when he spoke, was a low, raspy growl. "You're killing me, Em. Please understand."

"I've never felt like this before, Judd."

He groaned, then kissed her again, this time so soft and sweet, she trembled. He pressed his hips hard against her once, then forcibly pulled away. When he touched her cheek, his hand shook. "I'll call you later tonight, okay?"

She swallowed hard, not wanting him to leave, but knowing he was right. It *was* too soon to make a commitment.

It was difficult, but she managed to pull herself together. He was leaving; she knew that was for the best. But she had to recall what had started this whole argument and make certain he understood her position. "I was serious about what I said, Judd. I don't want you doing anything on your own. I don't want the...responsibility of your safety."

He pressed his forehead to hers and gave a loud sigh. "I know. I promise not to do anything until we've figured it all out." Then he chuckled, and it sounded so nice to her ears, she laughed, too. "I must be crazy." He gave her one more quick, hard kiss, then moved her away from the door. "I have to go before I forget my good intentions and ravish you right here. Any red-blooded male can only take so much provocation, you know. And honey, you're damn provoking."

She smiled again, and as he stepped out, Judd said, "Emily? Thanks again for breakfast."

Emily contained herself until she saw Judd drive away. Then she whirled and laughed. Her emotions had been on a roller coaster all day. Whether it had been good or bad, it had definitely been exciting. In fact, her time spent with Judd was easily the most exciting time she'd ever known.

He thought her provocative, and because of that, she felt provocative. That, too, was new, but decidedly delicious. She should feel guilty, since she hadn't done anything to help her brother yet. But she couldn't manage a single dollop of guilt. She simply felt too exhilarated.

HOURS LATER, Emily stood looking out her kitchen window, impatiently waiting for Judd's call. The house was dark and dim, just like her yard. She hadn't bothered to turn on the lights as she'd watched the sunset. The kitchen was her favorite room in the house. The pine cabinets had a warm golden hue, and the antique Tiffany lamp that hung over her table provided a touch of bright color. She thought of Judd sitting at that table with her, of the kiss he'd given her against the wall, and she wondered what he was up to, if he was safe...if he was with Suze.

That vagrant thought had her scowling, and she decided a soothing cup of chamomile tea was just what she needed. Without turning on the lights, she retrieved a cup from the cabinet and turned on the hot water. She knew her kitchen well and didn't need the light intruding on her warm, intimate mood.

It wasn't until she heard a sound and looked up that she realized she'd never reset the alarm. Her heart lodged in her throat as she saw a large body looming outside her kitchen door. Frozen in fear, she stood there as the hot water grew hotter and steam wafted upward around her face. A soft click sounded, and then another. When the door swung silently open and a man entered, his body a shadowed silhouette, she finally reacted. Emily let out the loudest ear-piercing scream she could manage. And after a stunned second and a low curse, the man pounced on her.

Emily didn't have time to run.

6

JUDD WHISTLED as he kicked off his shoes and dropped back onto the lumpy couch. God, it felt good to get off his feet. And to finally get home. He wanted to talk to Emily. He needed to make certain she'd understood his motives this afternoon. He'd seen the shock on her face, then the determination when she'd thought he was dumping her.

It had felt as if she'd snatched his heart right out of his chest. But what the hell else was he supposed to do? Watch her get involved? He hadn't counted on every guy around, including Donner, wanting to cozy up to her. He supposed that elusive sensuality he'd noticed in her right away was as visible to every other guy around as it was to him.

But he didn't like it. He didn't like other men looking at her and seeing tangled sheets and mussed hair and warm silky skin. He didn't like other guys thinking the thoughts he had.

He also couldn't hurt her. He'd just have to find a way to keep her close, and himself detached. That was going to be the real trick, especially when she did crazy things like offering him money just to keep him safe. He sure wasn't used to anyone trying to protect him, not since Max had been killed.

But he could get used to it, if he let himself.

His eyes narrowed at the thought. He couldn't get distracted from his purpose now, not when he was so close. Emily was a danger, and she didn't even realize it. She had the power to help him forget, and he didn't want that. Donner had hurt her brother, but he'd taken the only family Judd had ever known. Whenever he remembered Max's face, usually smiling, sometimes solemn, occasionally stern, his stomach tightened into a knot. Max was the finest, most honest person Judd had ever known, the only one who'd really cared about him.

Except for Emily.

Judd squeezed his eyes shut to block the thought. What Emily felt or didn't feel for him couldn't matter. Not now. Probably not ever. Judd wouldn't give up until Donner was put away. And after that, he'd have no more reason to be with her.

He was just reaching for the phone to call Emily, when the damn thing rang, causing him to jump. He snatched the receiver. "Yeah?"

"Judd, I'm glad I could reach you. Are you sitting down?"

Startled, it took Judd a second to answer. The lieutenant knew better than to call him at his apartment. It was a real breach of security. Something big must have happened. Trying to sound casual, he said, "As a matter of fact, I'd just propped my feet up. I've had a hell of a long—"

Howell interrupted. "Well, your day's about to get a whole lot longer." He hesitated, then added, "You remember that little lady you mentioned to me the other day? The rich one. She still hanging around with you?"

"Emily?" Judd didn't say that he couldn't forget her even if he tried. He cleared his throat. Even though he was as sure as he could be that no bugs existed in the apartment, he wouldn't take any chances. "Sure. In fact, I was just thinking about her. I guess we've got a regular thing going, at least for a while."

"I see." Judd could hear the restrained frustration in Howell's tone. "That being the case and all, I thought you ought to know, I just heard the little lady had her house broken into."

Judd felt his stomach lurch. "What?"

There was an expectant silence, then, "I recognize that tone, Judd. Just calm down and let me tell you what I know."

"Is Emily all right?"

"She's fine, just a little shaken up, I gather. It only happened a few minutes ago, but I thought... Judd?"

Judd cursed and pushed his feet back into his shoes, "I'm on my way."

He vaguely heard Howell protesting, and knew he'd catch hell later for hanging up on the lieutenant, but the only thought that mattered was seeing Emily. He raced out the front door, only stopping long enough to grab his jacket and his Beretta.

Ten minutes and three red lights later—which he ran—Judd decided he was too old to take this kind of stress. His palms were sweating and his head was pounding. He hadn't felt this kind of nauseating fear since the call telling him Max had been shot in the line of duty. But Judd hadn't made it then. He'd gotten to the hospital too late. Max had died only minutes before he arrived.

He stepped more firmly on the accelerator, pushing the old truck and thanking the powers that be for the near-empty roads that lessened the danger of his recklessness. His hands tightened on the wheel as his urgency increased. He could literally taste his fear.

When he sped into the curving driveway and saw the two black and whites parked there, he didn't stop to think about an excuse for his timely arrival. He simply busted through the door, his eyes searching until he found Emily.

She sat at the kitchen table holding an ice pack to her cheek. That alone was enough to make his blood freeze. She looked up, and the moment she saw him, her eyes widened, and then she smiled. "Judd."

He stalked toward her, sank to the floor beside her seat and took her hand in his. With his other hand, he lifted the ice pack so he could survey the damage. "Are you all right?"

She blinked away tears then glanced nervously at the hovering officers. "I'm fine, Judd. But how—"

Already her cheek was bruising and her eye was a bit puffy. Still holding her hand, Judd came to his feet and glared at the officers. "Who did this?"

"We don't know, Detective. We're still trying to find out all the details."

"Did you check the house? Has anyone searched the yard?" He didn't wait for an answer, but bent back to Emily. "Tell me what happened, honey."

She gave a nervous laugh, then quickly sobered. "Really, Judd, there's no reason to yell at the nice officers. They came almost as soon as I called."

"Why didn't you call me?"

He realized what a ridiculous question that was almost as soon as he made the demand. Emily thought he was a male stripper. Why would she call him? That fact had his temper rising again.

She leaned toward him and patted his shoulder. "Shh. It's all right, Judd. Just calm down."

She was trying to soothe him? Judd gave her a blank stare, then shook his head. "Emily..."

"I was waiting for your call. I guess after you left...I forgot to reset the alarm, because I was making tea when suddenly someone started opening the door."

"Oh, honey." Judd wrapped her in his arms, lifting her from the seat at the same time. "You must have been scared half to death."

Emily had to speak against his chest, since he was still holding her tight. He couldn't let her go just yet. He was still suffering from all the terrible thoughts that had raced through his head after Lieutenant Howell's call.

"I suppose I was scared at first," she said. "I know I screamed loud enough to startle the ducks on the lake. Then the man sort of just jumped toward me. And without really thinking about it, I turned the faucet sprayer on him." She leaned back to see Judd's face. "Do you remember me telling you the water heater was in need of repair? Well, I had the water running hot for my tea, and when he came at me, I just grabbed the hose and aimed at his face. At least, I think I hit his face. It was dark in here and everything happened so fast. I do know he yelled really loud, so I think the hot water must have hurt him."

Judd touched his fingers to her bruised cheek. "How did this happen?"

Emily looked very sheepish now, and her cheeks turned a bright pink. "It's really rather silly. You see, after the man yelled, I jerked away and ran for the library so I could use the phone. But, uh..." It was obvious to Judd she was embarrassed as her eyes again went to the two cops. "I tripped just inside the door. I hit my cheek on the leg of a chair."

Bemused, Judd asked, "The guy who broke in didn't do this to you?"

"No. I did it to myself. I think he left right after I shot him with the water. I locked the library door and called the police. When they got here, he was gone."

One of the cops cleared his throat. "We checked the water in her faucet. It's scalding hot. It's a wonder she hasn't burned herself before." Then he grinned. "You might want to get that checked."

Judd stared.

Emily pulled on his sleeve, regaining his attention. "Do you remember me telling you about my father burning his hand on the faucet? It really does get hot, hot enough to make tea without boiling the water. I wouldn't be at all surprised if the fellow has a serious burn on his face."

Feeling as though he'd walked into bedlam, Judd shook his head then turned his attention to the two officers. "Call Howell and tell him I'm spending the night here. And go check the area. With any luck, the bastard might still be out there if he's burned all that bad."

Both men nodded and started away. Judd turned to Emily, ready to lecture her on the importance of keeping her alarm set, when he felt her stiffen. She looked paper-white and her bottom lip trembled. He grabbed her arm and gently forced her back into her chair.

"Emily, I thought you said you were all right."

Her lips moved, but she didn't make a sound.

"Are you going to faint? Are you hurt somewhere?" He very carefully shook her. "Tell me what's wrong."

His urgency must have gotten through to her, for she suddenly cleared her throat, and her expression slowly changed to a suspicious frown. "One of the officers called you detective. And you're ordering them around as if you have the right. And even more ridiculous than that, they're letting you."

"Oh, hell." Judd wondered if there was any way for him to get out of this one. How could he have been so careless? Howell would surely have his head. His mind whirled with possible lies, but he couldn't see Emily believing any of them. She wasn't stupid, after all, just a bit naive.

He watched her face as he tried to come up with a logical, believable explanation, and he saw the confusion in her eyes, then the growing anger. One of the uniforms came around the corner and said, "Detective, I have Lieutenant Howell on the phone. He said he needed to talk to you, sir, uh...now." And Judd knew Emily had finally guessed the truth.

Before she could move, he cupped her cheeks, being especially gentle with her injury. "I can explain, honey. I swear. Just sit tight a second, okay? Right now, I have to pacify an enraged superior."

"Oh, I'll wait right here, Detective. You can count on it."

Judd didn't like the sound of that one little bit. But it was her look, one of mean anticipation, that had him frowning. This whole damn day had been screwy, starting with Emily cooking him breakfast. He should have known right then he wouldn't end it with his safe little world intact.

No, Emily had turned him upside down.

The hell of it was, he liked it.

EMILY LISTENED as Judd went through a long series of explanations over the phone. Yes, he could handle everything... No, his cover wasn't blown as long as Howell set things right with the two officers. Ha! His cover was most definitely *blown*. Emily wanted to interject at that point, but Judd watched her as he spoke, and so she kept herself still, her expression masked, she hoped.

Her cheek was still stinging, but not as much as her

pride. *Lord, Emily, you've been a fool.* Hadn't she known from the start that Judd didn't belong in the east side of Springfield? He talked the talk, and dressed the code, but something about him had been completely out of sync. He could be every bit as hard and cynical as the other roughnecks, but his behavior was forced. It wasn't something that came to him naturally.

She closed her eyes as she remembered offering him money to drop the case. If he reminded her of that, she just might...no. She would not lower herself to his level of deceit.

That decision did her little good when Judd hung up the phone and came back to kneel by her chair. He lifted the ice pack again and surveyed her bruised cheek with a worried frown. "I wonder if you should go to the hospital and have this checked."

"No."

Her curt response didn't put him off. "Does it hurt?"

"No."

His fingertips touched her, coasting over her abraded skin and causing goose bumps to rise on her arms. He ended by cupping her cheek and slowly rubbing his thumb over her lips. Then he sighed. "Just sit tight and I'll make you that tea. After everyone's cleared out, we'll talk."

Emily watched him bustle around the kitchen, thinking he looked curiously *right* there. It was almost as if the room had been built for his masculine presence.

The quarry-stone floor seemed every bit as sturdy and hard as Judd, the thick, polished pine cabinets just as comforting. There were no frilly curtains, no pastel colors to clash with his no-nonsense demeanor.

Emily made a disgusted face at herself. Comparing Judd to a kitchen? Maybe she had hit her head harder than she thought.

When he sat the tea in front of her, she accepted it with a mumbled thanks. Moments later, the officer who'd been outside came in and shook his head. "Not a sign of anything. It doesn't even look as if the door was tampered with."

Judd turned to Emily with a stern expression. "It was locked, wasn't it?"

Since she was already mortified over the evening's events, she didn't bother to try to hide her blush. "I really have no idea. I can't recall locking it, but sometimes I just do it by rote."

"Emily..."

She knew that tone. "Don't lecture me now, *Detective*. I'm really not in the mood."

She was saved from his annoyance by the remaining officer coming downstairs. "I checked out the other rooms. They're clean. I don't believe he ever left the kitchen. Probably took off right after she splashed him, going out the way he came in."

Judd worked his jaw. "I suppose you're right. You guys can take off now. I'll stay with Miss Cooper."

Since Emily had a lot of questions she wanted answered, she didn't refute him. It took the officers another five minutes to actually go, and then finally, she and Judd were alone. Sitting opposite him at the table,

Emily prepared to launch into her diatribe on the importance of honesty and to vent her feelings of abuse, when Judd spoke in a low, nearly inaudible tone.

"Clayton Donner shot Max about six months ago. I was out on assignment, and by the time I got to the hospital, Max was dead. I've made it my personal business to get Donner, and I'll damn well do whatever I have to until he's locked up."

Emily didn't move. She heard the unspoken words, telling her he wouldn't let her—or her feelings for him—get in his way. She'd thought she had a good personal reason to want Donner, but her motivation was nothing compared to Judd's. Without thinking, she reached out and took his hand. She didn't say a word, and after a few seconds, Judd continued.

"I told you Max had taken me in. He was everything to me, the only family I'd ever had. He was a regular street cop, and his run-in with Donner was pure coincidence. Max had only been doing a routine check on a disturbance, but he inadvertently got too close to the place where Donner was making a deal." Suddenly Judd's fist slammed down on the table and he squeezed his eyes shut.

"Judd?"

"Max got shot in the back." Judd drew a deep breath and squeezed Emily's hand. She squeezed back. He wouldn't look at her, but she could see his jaw was rigid, his eyes red. Her heart felt as though it were crumbling.

"We all knew it was Donner, but we couldn't get anything concrete on him. And to try him without enough evidence, and take the chance of letting him go free...I don't think I could stand it. I have to see him put away. Regardless of anything, or anyone, I'll get him."

Wishing he'd told her all this because he wanted to, not because he'd been forced, wouldn't get Emily anywhere. And she couldn't, in good conscience, interfere. Not when she could see how much getting Donner meant to him. "I understand."

"Do you?" For the first time, Judd looked up at her, and that look held so many different emotions, Emily couldn't begin to name them all. But the determination, the obsession, was clear, and it scared her. "I left everything behind when I followed Donner here," he said. "Springfield is just like my own home ground. Every city has an area with run-down housing and poverty, a place where kids are forgotten or ignored, where crime is commonplace and accepted. I fit in there, Em. I'm right at home. Sooner or later, I will get Donner. But not if you blow my cover. What happened tonight can't happen again."

Emily knew he wasn't talking about the break-in. "What—exactly—did happen, Judd?"

"I lost my head, and that's bad. I can't be sidetracked from this assignment."

"You know I want Donner, too."

"*Not like I do.*"

She would have liked to probe that a little more, but she held her tongue. She was afraid he was trying to find a way to say goodbye, to explain why he couldn't see her anymore. "What do you want me to do?"

Judd shot from his chair with an excess of energy. He shoved his hands into his back pockets and stalked the perimeter of the room as if seeking an escape. Finally, he stopped in front of the window, keeping his back to Emily. "I want you to understand that I can't let you get in my way. I can't...can't care about you. But when I think about what might have happened tonight..."

"You need me to stay out of your way?" Emily heard the trembling in her tone, but hoped Judd hadn't.

He whirled to face her. "No. Just the opposite, in fact."

She blinked twice and tried to still the frantic pounding of her pulse.

Again, Judd took his seat. "I work as a stripper in the bar because Donner does a lot of his business in the office upstairs. I've set myself up to get hired by him."

"That's what you were doing in the pool hall," Emily said with sudden insight. "You were impressing him, by being like him."

Judd nodded. "Everyone around there believes I'm out for a fast buck, a little fun, and not much else. That makes me Donner's ideal man. Making contact with him today was important. He'll be coming to me soon, I'm sure of it. He's intrigued, because he doesn't like people to refuse him, the way I refused him at the pool hall. I'd like to steer clear of you, to keep you uninvolved." He cast her a frustrated glance. "But it's too late for that."

Her stomach curled. "It is?"

One brisk nod was her answer. "I need you, Em. My superior thinks it's risky to make any changes now. He's already furious that you know my cover, but that can't be helped, short of calling everything off. And I don't want that. He'll pull the officers who were here tonight, because by rights, they screwed up, too. They shouldn't have acknowledged me as a detective, but they're rookies and..." He trailed off, then frowned at her. "If you suddenly stopped hanging around, after the scene we played out today at the pool hall, Donner might get suspicious. The whole deal could be blown. And it's too late for that."

Emily tried to look understanding, but she was still reacting to Judd's casual words. *He needs you, Emily.* She knew she would do whatever she could for him. "Has...has something come up? Something definite?"

"I think so. I visited Frog again after I left here. Next Wednesday night, Donner will be making a pickup."

"What kind of pickup?"

"He gets the guns dirt cheap since they're usually stolen. Then he sells them on the street for a much higher price. The man he buys from has a shipment ready. That would be the best time to bust him. In fact, it's probably the only way to make sure we nail him."

Seeing the determination in his eyes, Emily knew Judd would find a way to get Clayton Donner, with or without her help. But she wanted to be near him any way she could. "Since I still have my own reasons for wanting him caught, I'll be glad to help however I can."

She hesitated, then asked, "You're certain Donner is the one who sold my brother the gun?"

"As certain as I can be. We traced him to Springfield by the weapons he sold. One whole shipment was faulty guns. I don't know yet how Donner got hold of them, but from what you told me, it's safe to say your brother got one of them."

A resurgence of anger flooded through her. So Donner had known the guns were faulty before he sold them? He had deliberately risked her brother's life, and that fact made her determination almost equal to Judd's. "I look forward to doing whatever I can to help."

Judd let out a long breath. Then he leaned across the table and took both her hands. "I don't want to have to worry about you. I want your word that you won't try anything on your own. I don't even want you in that part of town without me. Promise me."

"I work there at the soup kitchen..."

"Not until this is over, Em. I mean it. It's just too risky. Promise me."

"Judd—"

"I lost Max, dammit! Isn't that enough?"

— His sudden loss of control shook her. She stared at his eyes, hard now with determination and an emotion that closely resembled fear. Reluctantly, she nodded. The last thing she wanted to do was distract him. Already, it seemed to her, he was too emotionally involved, and that weakened his objectivity, putting him in danger. It was obvious that Max Henley had been, and still was, the most important person in the world to Judd. Emily decided she might very well be able to keep an eye on Judd as long as he let her stay close. And evidently, the only way to do that, was to agree to his rules.

"All right. I promise. But I want a promise from you, too, Judd."

It took him a moment to regain his calm demeanor. Then he lifted an eyebrow in question.

"From now on, you have to be honest with me," she said. "There are few things I really abhor, but lying is one of them. You've lied to me from the start."

Judd turned his head. "I was on assignment, Em. And you just came tripping into my case, nearly messing everything up. I did what I thought was best."

"And of course telling me the truth never entered your mind?" When he gave her a severe frown, she quickly added, "Okay, not at first. But since then? Surely you had to realize I wasn't a threat?"

His stare was hard. "You're a bigger threat than you know."

Emily had no idea what that was supposed to mean. And while she did understand Judd's position, she couldn't help feeling like a fool. First she thought he was cop, then she believed he was a stripper. Now she finds out he actually is a cop. A small, humorless laugh escaped her. "I suppose it really is funny. Did you laugh at the irony of it, Judd?"

"Not once."

"Oh, come on. I must have looked like an idiot. And

here you were, trying to keep the poor naive little fool out of trouble."

"It wasn't like that, Em."

She stood, suddenly wanting to be alone. "I should have learned my lesson long ago." She knew Judd had no idea what she was talking about, that she was remembering her sad lack of judgment so many years ago. She shook her head, not at all certain she'd ever tell him. Lord, she probably wouldn't have the chance to tell him. Once this ordeal with Donner was over—and, according to Judd, it would be over soon—Judd would go on about his business, and she would have to forget about him.

"I wonder if my parents were right."

Judd hadn't moved. He sat in the chair watching her. "About what?"

"About me being such a bad judge of character. They always claim I have a very unrealistic perception of mankind, they say that I should accept the world, and my place in it, and stop trying to change things. I suppose I ought to give up and let them have their way."

Judd stiffened, and his expression looked dangerous. "You don't mean that."

With a shake of her head and another small smile, Emily turned to leave. Just before she reached the hallway entrance, she stopped. "One more thing, Judd."

She turned to face him and her gaze locked with his. "The man who came in here? He mumbled something, just before I ran, about only wanting the film."

Judd shot to his feet. "*What?*"

Her smile turned a bit crooked. "I didn't want to tell the police, because I thought it might be important. I was going to wait and tell you so we could figure out what the man meant. But now, since you are the police..." She shrugged.

Judd was busy cursing.

"What are you going to do?" she asked him.

"First, I'm going to get someone over here to check your door for fingerprints."

"It won't do any good. He wore gloves. I felt them when he grabbed me."

"Another tidbit you were saving only for me?"

"Uh-huh. I honestly don't know anything else, though." She stifled a forced yawn. "I think I'll get ready for bed now."

Judd moved to stand directly in front of her. "I'm staying the night, Em."

"That's not necessary." *But, oh, it would be so nice.* She sincerely hoped he would insist. For some reason, the thought of being all alone was very unsettling. And even more unsettling was the thought of letting Judd out of her sight.

"I think it is. I won't bother you, if that's what you're worried about."

"I wasn't worried."

He accepted that statement with a smile of his own. "Good. Why don't you show me where you want me to sleep? Then I've got a few more calls to make."

Since Emily wouldn't show him where she really wanted him to sleep, which was with her, she led him to the room down the hall from her bedroom. Decorated in muted shades of blue, it had only a twin bed and was considered her guest room. There were two other bedrooms, one was John's room, since he dropped in often whenever there were problems with her parents, and the other room served as a small upstairs sitting room.

Judd nodded his approval, then took Emily's shoulders. "Try to sleep. But honey, if you need anything, don't hesitate to let me know."

He doesn't mean what you're thinking, Em. Didn't he just tell you earlier tonight it was too soon? "Thank you, Judd. Good night." Emily forced her feet to move down the hall, then she forced herself inside her room and closed the door. Her forehead made a soft *thwack* when she dropped it against the wood, and her cheek started throbbing again.

But none of it was as apparent as the drumming of her heart. It was all just beginning to sink in, from the slapstick beginning to the frightening end. Judd was an officer, who chose to take his clothes off in an undercover case, using a police uniform as a costume. It was too ironic. And Lord help her, so was her situation.

She was falling in love with a thoroughly outrageous man.

JUDD LAY in the narrow bed, stripped down to his underwear, with only the sheet covering him. His arms were propped behind his head and he listened to the strange sounds of the house as it settled. He'd left the door open in case Emily needed him.

God, what a mess.

Howell had raised holy hell with him, and for good reason. He'd behaved like a rookie with no experience at all. He knew better, hell, he was damn good at his job. But he just kept thinking of what could have happened. The thought of Emily being hurt was untenable. He had to find some way to wrap this operation up, and quickly. He didn't want to be involved with her, didn't want to care about her. But he knew it was too late.

Did two people ever come from more different backgrounds? Emily was cultured, refined, elegant. She had a poise that never seemed to leave her, and a way of talking that implied gentleness and kindness and...all the things he wasn't. That refined speech of hers turned him on. Everything about her turned him on.

He had to quell those thoughts. Emily wasn't for him. From what he knew of her parents, they would balk at the mere mention of her getting involved with someone like him. And he didn't want to add to her problems there. She evidently had some very real differences with her parents, but at least she had parents. And probably aunts and uncles and grandparents, all of them educated and smelling of old money.

The only smells Judd had been familiar with around his house were stale beer and unwashed dishes. Max had tried to teach him a better way, but Max had been a simple man with simple manners. He hadn't owned a speck of real silver, yet that was exactly what Emily stirred her tea with. And he couldn't be certain, but he thought the teacup she'd used earlier was authentic china. It had seemed delicate and fragile—just like Emily.

He squeezed his eyes shut, trying to close out the image of her lying soft and warm in her own bed, her dark hair fanned out on the pillow, those big brown eyes sleepy, her skin flushed. He wanted her, more than he'd ever wanted anything in his life. He hadn't known a man could want this much and live through it. She was right down the hall, and he suspected if he went to her, she wouldn't send him away.

But as bad as he wanted her, he also knew he had no right to her. So he continued to stare at the ceiling.

Somewhere downstairs he heard a clock chime eleven. Then he heard a different noise, one he hadn't heard yet, and he turned his head on the pillow to look toward the door.

Emily stood there, a slight form silhouetted by the vague light of the moon coming through the window. He couldn't quite draw a breath deep enough to chase away the tightness in his chest. When she didn't move, he leaned up on one elbow. His voice sounded low and rough when he spoke. "Are you all right, babe?"

She made another small, helpless sound, then took a tiny step into the room. Every muscle in his body tensed.

He couldn't make out her face, but he could tell her gown was long and pale and he could feel her nervousness. He didn't know why she was here, but his body had a few ideas and was reacting accordingly. He was instantly and painfully aroused. "Em?"

She took another step, then whispered in a trembling tone, "I know you said it was too soon. And you're right, of course. I told myself this wasn't proper, that I should behave with some decorum." Her hands twisted together and she drew a deep, shaky breath. "But you see, the thing is..."

Judd knew his heart was going to slam right through his ribs. He couldn't wait another second for her to finish her sketchy explanation. She was here, she wanted him, and despite all the reasons he'd just given himself for why he shouldn't, he knew he wanted her too badly to send her away.

He stared at her in the darkness, and then lifted the sheet. "Come here, Emily."

7

SHE MOVED SO FAST, Judd barely had time to brace himself for her weight. Not that she weighed anything at all. She was soft and sweet and she smelled so incredibly inviting—like a woman aroused. Like feminine heat and excitement. Her brushed-cotton gown tangled around his legs when he turned and pinned her beneath him. He felt her body sigh into his, her slim legs parting, her pelvis arching up. In the next instant, her hands cupped his face and she kissed him. It wasn't a gentle kiss. She ate at his mouth, hungry and anxious and needy.

So many feelings swamped him. Lust, of course, since Emily always inspired that base craving, even when she wasn't intent on seducing him. And need, a need he didn't like acknowledging, but one that was so powerful, so all-consuming, he couldn't minimize it as anything less than what it was.

But first and foremost was tenderness, laced with a touch of relief that he wouldn't have to pull back this time; she would finally be his. She had come to him, and she was kissing him as if she wanted him every bit as badly as he wanted her. That wasn't possible, but if her need was anywhere close to his, they both might damn well explode.

"Emily..."

Her kisses, hot and urgent, landed against his jaw, his chin, the side of his mouth. Her nipples were taut against his chest, her breath hot and fast. He wanted to touch her everywhere, all at once, and he wanted to simply hold her, to let her know how precious she was. He slid one hand down her side, felt her shiver, heard her moan, and he nearly lost his mind. He gripped her small backside with both hands and urged her higher against his throbbing erection, rubbing sinuously, slow and deep, again and again. He wanted to drown in the hot friction, the sensual feel of her warm body giving way to him. Her legs parted wide and she bent her knees, cradling him, offering herself.

Judd groaned low in his throat and went still, aware of the soft heat between her thighs now touching him. He knew she was excited, and the fact was making him crazy. "Too fast, honey. Way too fast."

Emily wasn't listening. Her hands frantically stroked his naked back and her legs shifted restlessly, rubbing against his, holding him. She continued to lift her hips into him, exciting herself, exciting him more. Judd dropped his full weight on her to keep her still, then carefully caged her face. She whimpered, trying to move.

"Shh. It's all right, Em. We've got all night." Then he kissed her. She tasted hot and sweet, and when he slipped his tongue between her lips, she sucked on him with greedy excitement.

Judd had never known kissing to be such a deeply sensual experience. To him, it had always been pleasant, sometimes a prelude to sex, sometimes not. But he'd never felt such a keen desire just from kissing. Emily was driving him over the edge, and he hadn't even touched her yet.

He caught her slim wrists in one hand and trapped them over her head. He had to take control or he'd never last. She muttered a low protest and her hips moved, rubbing and seeking beneath his, finding his erection and grinding against it. Her nightgown was in his way and he knotted one fist in the material and lifted, urgently. He needed to touch all of her, to explore her body, to brand her as his own. Emily squirmed to accommodate him, allowing the material to be jerked above her waist. When Judd felt her bare, slender thighs against his own, he growled and pushed against her.

It almost struck him as funny, the effect she had on him. Prim, polite, proper little Emily. He dipped his head and nuzzled her breasts at the same time he slid his hand over her silky mound, letting his fingers tangle in her damp curls. Emily stopped moving; she even stopped breathing. Judd felt her suspended anticipation.

He released her wrists long enough to jerk the buttons open on the bodice of her nightgown so he could taste her nipples, feel the heat of her flesh, and then he wedged his hand back between her thighs. He pressed his face to her breast and kissed her soft skin, his mouth open and wet. Emily shifted so her puckered nipple brushed against his cheek and Judd smiled, then began to suckle, drawing her in deep, stroking with his tongue, nipping with his teeth.

Her ragged moan was low and so damn sexy he moaned with her. His fingers slid over the tight curls, felt her slick and wet, hot and swollen with wanting him, and then he slid a finger deep inside her. She was incredibly tight and he added another finger, hearing her groan, feeling her body clasp his fingers as he forced them a bit deeper, stretching her.

He began a smooth rhythm, and with a breathless moan, her body moved with him. His thumb lifted to glide over the apex of her mound, finding her most sensitive flesh and stroking it, while his mouth still drew greedily on her nipple, and Emily suddenly stiffened, then screamed out her climax. Judd went still with shock.

Her slim body shuddered and lifted beneath his, her face pulled tight in her pleasure. He watched her every movement, her intense delight expressed in her narrowed eyes, her parted lips, the sweet sounds she made. Judd knew he had never seen anything so beautiful, so right. It seemed to go on and on, and as her cries turned to low breathless moans, he kissed her, taking her pleasure into himself.

When she stilled, he continued to cuddle her close, his own need now put on hold. A tenderness he'd never experienced before swirled through him, and he couldn't help smiling. Miss Cooper was a red-hot fire-cracker, and he must be the luckiest man alive. "You okay, Em?"

She didn't answer. Her breasts were still heaving and her heartbeat thundered against his chest. Judd placed one last gentle kiss on her open mouth, then lifted him-self away to reach for his pants. He fumbled in the pockets until he found his wallet and located a condom. When he turned back to Emily, he saw her watching him, her dark eyes so wide they filled her face. Her bot-tom lip trembled as she slowly drew in uneven breaths. Damp curls framed her face and her expression was wary.

She was probably a bit embarrassed by her unre-strained display. He didn't have time to soothe her, though. He needed to be inside her, right now, feeling her body clasped tight around his erection just as it had clasped his fingers. With the help of the moonlight, he could see her pale belly and still-open thighs. He bent and pressed his mouth to her moist female flesh, breathing in her scent and his need for her over-whelmed him. His tongue flicked out, stroking her, rasping over her delicate tissues and he gained one small taste of her excitement before Emily gasped and began struggling away.

He caught the hem of her gown and wrestled it over her head, chuckling at the way she tried to stop him. She slapped at his hands, and when she realized he had won the tug-of-war, she covered her face with her

hands. Once the gown was free, Judd tossed it aside
and then immediately pulled her hands away from her
face. The feel of her naked body, so warm and soft and
ready, made him shudder. He covered her completely
and said in the same breath, "You are so beautiful, Em.
I've never known a woman like you."

She peeked one eye open and studied him. "Really?"

"Oh, yes," he answered in his most fervent tone.

She said a small, "Oh," and then he lifted her knees
with his hands, spread her legs wide and pushed inside
her. She was tight and hot and so wet... Slowly, her
body accepted his length, taking him in by inches, her
softness giving way to his hardness. Judd had to clench
his teeth and strain for control. She made small sounds
of distress, and he knew he was stretching her, but she
didn't fight him, didn't push him away. Her small
hands clenched on his shoulders and held him close.

It didn't take her long to forget her embarrassment
once he was fully inside her. He ground against her, his
gaze holding her own, seeing her eyes go hot and dark
and intent. She pulled her bottom lip between her teeth
and arched her neck.

"That's it, sweetheart." He drew a deep breath and
began moving. Emily rocked against him, meeting his
rhythm, holding him tight. He pressed his lips to her
neck, breathing in her scent. He slid his hands down her
back and cupped her soft bottom, lifting her higher. He
felt her nipples rasp against his chest. Every touch,
every breath, seemed to heighten his arousal. When she
tightened her thighs and sobbed, her internal muscles

milking his erection until he wanted to die, he gave up any effort at control and climaxed with a low, rough endless growl.

It took him a few minutes to realize he was probably squashing Emily. She didn't complain, but then, she wouldn't.

He lifted up and stared at her face. His eyes had adjusted to the darkness, and he could see her fine, dark hair lying in disheveled curls on the pillow. Her eyes were closed, her lashes weaving long thick shadows across her cheeks. The whiteness of her breasts reflected the moonlight, and Judd couldn't resist leaning down to softly lathe a smooth, pink nipple. It immediately puckered.

He smiled and blew against her skin.

Emily squirmed. "You're still inside me."

"Mmm. I'm still hard, too."

"I noticed."

Her shy, quiet voice touched him and he smoothed her hair away from her forehead. "I've wanted you a long time, Emily."

"We haven't known each other a long time."

She still hadn't opened her eyes. He kissed the tip of her nose. "I've wanted you for as long as I can remember. It doesn't matter that we hadn't met yet." She shivered and Judd touched his tongue to her shoulder. "Your skin is so damn soft and smooth. I love touching you. And tasting you."

He licked a path up her throat, then over to her earlobe. "I could stay like this forever."

Emily drew in a shuddering breath. "No, you couldn't."

He laughed, knowing she'd felt the involuntary flex of his erection deep inside her. He wanted her again. "If I get another condom, do you promise to stay exactly like this?"

"Will you let me touch you a little this time, too?"

His stomach tightened at the thought. And he hurriedly searched through the wallet he'd tossed on the floor only minutes earlier.

But once he was ready, he still couldn't let Emily have her way. Watching her react, touching her and seeing his effect on her, was stimulant enough. He'd thought to go slowly this time, to savor his time with her. But every little sound she made drove him closer to the edge. And when he entered her, the friction felt so unbearably good, he knew he wouldn't be able to slow down.

He'd told her the truth. He'd been waiting for her forever. But now he had her, and he didn't want to let her go.

EMILY WOKE the next day feeling fuzzy and warm and remarkably content. Then she realized Judd was beside her, one arm thrown over her hips, his face pressed into her breasts. His chest hair tickled her belly and their legs were entwined. They were both buck naked.

She should have been appalled, but seeing Judd looking so vulnerable, his hair mussed, his face relaxed, made her heart swell with emotion. Very carefully, so she wouldn't awaken him, she sifted her fingers through his hair. It felt cool and silky soft. Emily wouldn't have guessed there was anything soft about Judd. She placed a very careful kiss on his crown.

He shifted slightly, nuzzling closer to her breasts and she held her breath. But he continued sleeping. She was used to seeing the shadow of a beard on his face, but feeling it against her tender skin added something to the experience. She looked down the length of their bodies, and the vivid contrast excited her. He was so dark, so hard and muscled, while she was smooth and pale and seemed nearly fragile beside him.

She almost wished he would wake up, but he appeared totally exhausted. His breathing was deep and even, and when she slipped away from him, he merely grumbled a complaint and rolled over onto his back.

Lord help him. The man did have a fine body. It was certainly shameful of her to stand there leering at him, but she couldn't quite pull her eyes away. Dark hair covered his body in very strategic places, sometimes concealing, sometimes enhancing his masculinity. And Judd Sanders was most definitely masculine. He took her breath away.

Emily might have stood there gawking until he did wake up, if she hadn't heard a knock on her front door. She gave a guilty start, her hand going to her throat, before she realized Judd had slept through the sound, and the person at the door had no notion she was presently entertaining herself with the sight of a naked man.

She snatched her gown, then ran to her own bedroom

to retrieve the matching robe. By the time she got downstairs, the knocking had become much louder. "Just a minute," she mumbled.

When she peeked out the small window in the door, she couldn't have been more surprised. For the longest moment, she simply stood there, crying and laughing. When her brother shook his head and laughed back, she remembered to open the door and let him in.

She grabbed him into her arms, even though he stood much taller than herself, and squeezed him as tight as she could. She couldn't stem the tide of tears, and didn't bother trying. "Oh, John, it's so good to see you."

"You, too, Emmie. What took you so long to let me in?"

Emily froze. Uh-oh.

"Emmie? Hey, what's up?"

She shook her head. "What are you doing here, John? I thought you were still out of the country. Did Mother and Father come with you?"

He set two suitcases just inside the door then walked past her, heading for the kitchen. Ever since she'd bought the house, the kitchen had become a kind of informal meeting place. Whenever John visited, they sat at the kitchen table and talked until late into the night.

"John?"

"Could I have something to drink first, Em? It's been a long trip."

Emily stared at John, trying to be objective. He looked better, so much better. The scars on his right temple and upper cheek had diminished, and now only a thin, jagged line cut through his eyebrow. He'd healed nicely, but his eyes still worried her. They seemed tired and sad and...hopeless.

"You look wonderful, John. The plastic surgeons did a great job."

He scoffed. "You call this a great job? This is as good as it gets, Em, though Mom keeps insisting she'll find a better surgeon who'll make me look as 'good as new.' She refuses to believe nothing more can be done."

Emily closed her eyes, wondering why her mother couldn't see the hurt she caused with such careless comments. "John, I never thought the scars were that bad. I was more concerned about your eyesight, and once we realized there wouldn't be any permanent damage there, I was grateful. You should be, too."

"Oh, yeah. I'm real grateful to look like a freak."

For one of the few times in her life, Emily lost her temper with her baby brother. It was so rare for her to be angry with John, she almost didn't recognize the feeling. And then she slammed her hand onto the counter and whirled to face him. "Don't you ever say something so horrible again! You're my brother, dammit, and I love you. You are not a freak."

John seemed stunned by her display. He sat there, silently watching her, his dark eyes round, his body still. Emily covered her mouth with her hand and tried to collect her emotions. Then she cleared her throat. "Are you hungry?"

A small, relieved smile quirked on his lips. "Yeah, a little."

"I'll start breakfast. The coffee should be ready in just a minute. There's also juice in the refrigerator."

John tilted his head. "Since when do you drink coffee? The last time I asked, you said it was bad for me and gave me tea instead."

"Uh..." She'd bought the coffee for Judd, but it didn't seem prudent to tell John that. "You're older now. I see no reason why you can't drink coffee if you like."

"Okay." John still seemed a little bemused, but then he squared his shoulders. "I ran away, Emmie. Mom and Dad refused to bring me home, and I couldn't take another minute of sitting around waiting to see which doctor they'd produce next."

Suddenly, Emily felt so tired she wanted to collapse. "They'll be worried sick, John."

"Ha! I left them a note. You watch. When they can't reach me at home, they'll call here, probably blame you somehow, then carry on as if they're on vacation. We both know they'll be glad to be rid of me. Lately, I've been an *embarrassment*."

Since Emily had suffered similarly at the hands of her parents, she knew she couldn't truthfully deny what he said. She decided to stick to the facts, and to try to figure out what to do. "You came straight here from the airport?"

"Yeah. Mom and Dad probably don't even realize I'm gone yet. They had a couple of parties to attend."

The disdain, and the hurt, were obvious in his tone. She wished she could make it all better for John, but she didn't have any answers. "You know you're welcome here as long as you like."

John stared at his feet. "Thanks."

"You also know you'll have to face them again sooner or later."

"I don't see why," he said. "They're disgusted with me now, but they won't say so. They never really say anything. You know how they are. I won't hang around and let them treat me the way they treat you. Do you remember how they acted when that fiancé of yours tried to scam them for money? Did they offer you support or comfort? No, they wouldn't even come right out and yell at you. They just made you feel like dirt. And they never forget. I don't think you've been to the house since, that Mom didn't manage to bring it up, always in some polite way, that she'd been right all along about him, that you'd been used by that jerk, just so he could get his hands on your money." John shook his head. "No thanks, I don't want to put up with that. I can just imagine...how...I'd..."

Emily looked up from pouring the coffee when John's voice trailed off. She'd heard it all before, his anger on her behalf, his indignation that she let her parents indulge in their little barbs.

She didn't understand what had silenced him now until she followed his gaze and saw Judd leaning against the doorjamb. He had his jeans on—just barely. The top button was undone and they rode low on his hips. His feet were bare, he wore no shirt and his hair fell over his forehead in disarray. He looked incredibly sexy, and the way he watched her, with so much heat, instantly had her blushing.

Then John stood. "Who the hell are you, and what are you doing in my sister's house?"

JUDD WISHED Emily's little brother had waited just a bit longer before noticing him. The conversation had taken a rather interesting turn, and he wouldn't have minded gaining a little more insight into Emily. But he supposed he could question her later on this fiancé of hers and find out exactly what had happened.

He was careful not to look overlong at the boy's scars, not that they were really all that noticeable, anyway. But just from the little he'd heard, he knew John was very sensitive about them. He was actually a good-looking kid, with the all-American look of wealth. Now, however, he appeared mightily provoked and ready to attack.

Judd ignored him.

His gaze locked on Emily, and suddenly he was cursing. "Damn, Em, are you okay?"

Emily faltered. "What?"

He strode forward until he could gently touch the side of her face. "You've got a black eye."

"I do?" Her hand went instantly to her cheek.

"It's not bad, babe. But it looks like it might hurt like hell."

She cleared her throat and cast a nervous glance at her brother. "No, it feels fine."

Judd smiled, then deliberately leaned down to press

a gentle kiss to the bruise. Before Emily could step away, he caught her hands and lifted them out to her sides. In a low, husky tone, he said, "Look at you." His eyes skimmed over the white cotton eyelet robe. The hem of her gown was visible beneath and showed a row of lace and ice-blue satin trim. It was feminine and romantic and had him hard in a heartbeat.

Leaning down by her ear, Judd whispered in a low tone so her brother wouldn't hear, "I woke up and missed you. You shouldn't have left me."

He could feel the heat of her blush and smiled to himself, then turned to greet her brother. The kid looked about to self-destruct. Judd stuck out his hand. "Hi. Judd Sanders."

John glared. "What are you doing in my sister's house?" he repeated.

"That's none of your damn business." Then in the next breath, Judd asked, "Didn't you notice Emily's black eye?"

John stiffened, a guilty flush staining his lean cheeks. "It's not that noticeable. And besides, Emily was asking about me, so I didn't have time—"

"Yeah, right." Judd turned to Emily. "Why don't you sit down and rest? I'll fix breakfast. What do you feel like eating?"

"Hey, wait a minute!" John's neck had turned red now, too. He apparently didn't like being ignored.

Judd sighed. "What?"

For a moment, John seemed to forget what he wanted. He opened his mouth twice, and his hand went self-consciously to his scar. Then he asked, with a good dose of suspicion, "How did Emmie get a black eye?"

Judd smiled to himself. He folded his arms over his chest and braced his bare feet apart. "Some guy broke in here—"

"It was nothing, John." Emily frowned at Judd and then rushed toward her brother. "Would you like to go freshen up, John, before breakfast?"

"Women freshen up, Em. Not men."

She glared at Judd for that observation.

Judd lifted his eyebrow. "He has every right to know what happened to you. He's your brother and you care about him, so it only stands to reason that he cares for you, too." Judd looked toward John. "Am I right?"

"Yeah." John stepped forward. "What did happen?"

Emily looked so harassed, Judd took pity on her. "Why don't you go upstairs and...freshen up, Em, or change or whatever. I'll entertain your brother for you and start breakfast." Then he leaned down close to her ear. "Not that I don't like what you're wearing. You look damn sexy. But little brother looks ready to attack."

Her eyes widened and she cast a quick glance at John. "Yes, well, I suppose I ought to get dressed..." She rushed from the room. Judd watched her go, admiring the way her delectable rear swayed in the soft gown.

"What did you say to her?"

Little brothers were apparently a pain in the butt, and Judd wasn't known for his patience. But he supposed, for Emily, he ought to make the effort. "I told her how attractive she is. I get the feeling she isn't used to hearing compliments very often." The way he said it placed part of the blame for that condition directly on John. Judd didn't think it would hurt him to know Emily needed comforting every bit as much as anyone else. "Emily's a woman. They like to know when they look nice."

As he spoke, Judd opened the cabinets and rummaged around for pancake mix and syrup. It was one of the few breakfast things he knew how to make. He wanted to pamper Emily, to make her realize how special she was.

Last night had been unexpected, something he hadn't dared dream about, something he supposed shouldn't have happened. But it had happened, and even though he didn't know what he was going to do about it yet, how to balance his feelings for Emily with his need to get Donner, he knew he didn't want her to be uncomfortable around him.

He thought breakfast might be a good start. Besides, he owed her one from yesterday.

John interrupted his thoughts with a lot of grousing and grumbling. "I'm good to Emily."

"Are you?" He pulled out a couple of eggs to put in the mix, his mind whirling on possible ways to proceed against Donner, while keeping Emily uninvolved. Perhaps having her brother here would distract her from capturing the gun dealer.

"She's been worried about me."

Judd glanced at John as he pulled down a large glass

mixing bowl. "I don't see why. You seem healthy and strong. Hell, you're twice her size." He took the milk from the refrigerator and added it to the mix.

"I nearly lost my eyesight not too long ago. And now I've got these damn scars."

Judd gave up for a moment on the pancakes. He turned to give John his full attention. "That little scar on the side of your face?"

John nearly choked. "Little?"

"It's not that big a deal. So you've got a scar? You're a man. Men are expected to get banged up a little. Happens all the time. It's not like you're disabled or anything. You'll still be able to work and support yourself, won't you?"

"I'm only sixteen."

Judd shrugged. "I was thinking long term."

"My face is ruined."

"Naw. You're still a good-lookin' kid. And in a few more years, that scar will most likely fade until you can barely see it. Besides, you'll probably get all kinds of sympathy from the females once you hit college. So what's the problem?"

John collapsed back in his chair. "You really don't think the scars are all that bad?"

Judd went back to mixing the batter. "I didn't even notice them at first. Of course, with Emily around that's not saying much. I wouldn't notice an elephant at the table when she looks at me with those big brown eyes. Your sister is a real charmer."

There was a stretch of silence. "You and Emily got something going?"

"Yeah. Something. I'm not sure what. Hey, how many pancakes can you eat? About ten?"

"I suppose. I didn't know Emily was dating anyone."

"We aren't actually dating."

"Oh." Another silence. "Should I be worried about this?"

That brought Judd around. "Well, hallelujah. I didn't think anyone ever worried about Em."

John frowned. "She's my sister. Of course I worry about her."

"Good. But no, you don't have to worry right now. I'll take care of her."

"And I'm just supposed to believe you because you say so?"

He almost smiled again. John sounded just like his sister. "Why not? Emily does."

That brought a laugh. "My parents would have a field day with that analogy. They don't think Emily has very good judgment."

"And what do you think?"

"I think she's too naive, too trusting and a very good person."

Judd grinned. "Me, too."

"So tell me how she got the black eye."

Suddenly, John looked much older, and very serious. Judd gave one sharp nod. "You can set the table while I talk."

Fifteen minutes later, Judd had three plates full of

pancakes, and he'd finished a rather convoluted explanation of Emily's exploits. It was an abridged version, because even though Judd admitted to helping Emily, he didn't say anything about going undercover as a male stripper, or his overwhelming attraction to Emily, or their newly discovered sexual chemistry. In fact, he wasn't certain yet just what that chemistry was, so he sure as hell wasn't about to discuss it with anyone, let alone Emily's little brother.

John was appalled to learn what steps Emily had taken to try to help him.

And he hadn't even noticed her black eye.

Judd knew he was feeling guilty, which hopefully would help bring him out of his self-pity. "So you can see how serious Emily is about this."

"Damn." John rubbed one hand over his scar, then across his neck. "What can I do to help?"

Ah. Just the reaction he'd hoped for. From what Emily had told him about John, Judd hadn't known for sure what to expect. By all accounts, John could have been a very spoiled, selfish punk. But then, he had Emily for a sister, so that scenario didn't seem entirely feasible. "You want to help? Stay out of the east end. And stay out of trouble."

"But there must be something—"

"No." When John started to object, Judd cursed. "I'm having enough trouble keeping an eye on Emily. And she has enough to do without worrying about you more than she already does. Give her a rest, John. Get your act together and keep it together."

"That's easy for you to say. You don't know my parents."

"No. But I do know your sister. If she turned out so great, I suppose you can, too."

John laughed. "That's one way of looking at it."

Emily walked into the room just then, and Judd immediately went to her. He tried to keep his eyes on her face as he talked to her, but she was wearing another one of those soft, ladylike dresses. But what really drove him insane was the white lace tie that circled her throat and ended in a bow. Without meaning to, his fingers began toying with it. "I told your brother what happened."

The frown she gave him showed both irritation and concern. "Judd."

"Hey, it's okay," John said as he took a plate of pancakes and smothered them in warm syrup. "I'm glad he told me. And I'm glad he's looking after you."

"Judd is not looking after me. He's a...well, a partner of sorts."

Judd lowered his eyebrows as if in deep thought, then gave a slow, very serious nod. "Of sorts."

The look she sent him insisted he behave himself. He wasn't going to, though. A slight tug on the bow brought her an inch or two closer. His eyes drifted from her neatly brushed hair, her slender stockinged legs and her flat, black shoes. Her attire was casual, but also very elegant. "You look real pretty in that dress, Em. Do you always wear such...feminine stuff?"

Trying to act as though she wasn't flushed a bright

pink, Emily stepped out of his reach and picked up her own plate. She stared at the huge stack of pancakes. "Most of my wardrobe is similar, yes. This is one of my older dresses because I have some work to do today."

"I like it."

John suddenly laughed. "I think you've caught a live one, Emmie. I don't remember what's-his-name ever acting this outrageous. He always tried to suck up to Mom and Dad by being as stuffy and proper as they are."

After frowning at her brother and giving a quick shake of her head, she said, "I can't truly imagine Judd ever 'sucking up' to anyone. Can you?"

"It'll be interesting to see what the folks think of him."

An expression of horror passed over her face. "For heaven's sake, John. I doubt Judd has any interest in meeting our parents."

Judd narrowed his eyes at the way she'd said that. So she didn't want him to meet them? It was no skin off his nose. He wasn't into doing the family thing, anyway. He couldn't remember one single woman he'd ever dated who wanted to rush him home to meet her mama.

But somehow, coming from Emily, the implicit rejection smarted. "There wouldn't be any reason for me to meet them. Especially since they're out of the country, right?"

Emily stared at her fork. "Yes. And we should have

everything resolved before they return if we're as close to finishing this business as you say."

And once everything was resolved, there would be no reason to keep him around? Judd wanted to ask, but he couldn't. It was annoying to admit, but he felt vulnerable. He couldn't quite credit Emily with using him; she simply wasn't that mercenary. But that didn't mean she wouldn't gladly take advantage of a situation when it presented itself. He'd known from the start that she wanted him. They'd met, and sparks had shot off all around them. And if she wanted to have a fling on what she considered "the wild side of life," Judd was more than willing to oblige. For a time.

He would get a great deal of satisfaction when Donner was taken care of, and he'd be able to return to his normal routine: life without a driving purpose. He'd be alone again, without Max and without the overwhelming need to avenge him. Actually, he'd have no commitments, no obligations at all, unless Emily...

Judd shook his head. With any luck, he'd be wrong in what he was feeling, and he wouldn't miss her. The time he had with Emily right now would be enough.

Hell, he'd make it enough.

With that thought in mind, he urged Emily to eat, and he dug into his own pancakes. When she was almost finished, curiosity got the better of him and he asked, "So who was this bozo who tried to schmooze your parents?"

Emily choked. He took the time to whack her on the

back a few times, then caught her chin and turned her face his way. "Emily?"

When she didn't answer right away, John spoke up. "Emmie was engaged to a guy for a while. She loved him, but he only wanted to use her to get in good with my parents. Luckily, everyone found out in time, before the wedding."

"Thank you very much, John."

"Oh, come on, sis. It wasn't your fault. The guy was a con artist."

"Yes, he was. And that is all in the past. I'd appreciate it if we found something else to talk about."

Judd transferred his gaze to John. "Your folks are pretty hard on her about it still?"

"God, yes. And she lets them. I don't think I've ever heard her really defend herself, though I'd like to see her tell them where to go. They even try to bully her into giving up her work with the homeless. They keep reminding her how she got burned once. It was a real embarrassing event. The papers got wind of it and all of society knew." John made a face, then added, "My parents really hate being publicly embarrassed."

With a disgusted sound of protest, Emily stood and took her plate to the sink. Judd glanced toward her, then back to John. "She's still a little touchy about it."

"Yeah. It was pretty hard on her. But Emmie is tough, and she doesn't let anything really get her down. Including Mom and Dad. That's why she moved here, away from my folks. She won't argue with them, but she will walk away. Of course, they hate this house, too. I don't know why she puts up with them."

Swiveling in his chair, Judd saw the stiff set to Emily's shoulders, the way she clenched her hands on the sink counter. He wanted to hold her, to comfort her, but the time wasn't right. Later, though... "Did you love him, Em?"

It took her so long to answer, Judd thought she'd decided to ignore him. It wasn't any of his business, but he wanted to know. The thought of her still pining over some guy didn't sit right with him.

Then she finally shook her head. "I suppose I thought I did...maybe I did. But now, it doesn't seem like I could have. I was so wrong about him. He was out of work and needed me, and I thought he cared about me, too. But he turned out to be a really horrible man."

Judd was out of his seat and standing behind her in a heartbeat. "That was one incident."

She turned and smiled at him. "Are you thinking I might decide I was wrong about you, too, Detective?"

"Since I don't know what you think about me, how am I supposed to answer that?"

When it came, her smile was sweet enough and warm enough to make his muscles clench. He caged her waist between his hands and waited.

"I think you're probably a real-life hero, Judd, and unlike any man I've ever known."

The words hit him like a blow. He stared into her dark eyes, dumbfounded. He saw her acceptance, her giving. He was a man with no family, no ties, a cop out to do a job, and willing to use her to do it. He was certainly no hero. But if that was what Emily wanted...

John cleared his throat. "Maybe I should make myself scarce."

Remembering where they were and who was with them, Judd forced himself to release Emily and take two steps back—away from temptation. "No. You can help me do the dishes while Emily calls to see if she can get someone here to repair the hot-water heater."

"Do the dishes? But I don't know how..."

Judd smirked. "It's easy. I'll show you what to do."

"But—"

"Do you want to be able to take care of yourself or not?"

Emily laughed. "Well put. I'll leave you two to tend to your chores." But she stopped at the doorway. "By the way, Judd. What if there was something on that film?"

"I'm picking it up today. Then we'll know."

"I'll go with you."

"No, you won't."

"But..."

His sigh was exaggerated. "You're as bad as your brother, Em. I thought we had an agreement."

When she turned around and practically stomped away without a word, Judd decided she was mad. "Well, hell."

John only laughed. "Gee, I'm really tired. Too much traveling, I guess. I think I might need to spend a lot of time in my room, resting up."

"What's that supposed to mean?"

With a buddy-type punch in the shoulder, John said, "I think you're going to have your hands full with Emmie. She can be as stubborn as a mule, and it's no telling who will win. I don't want to get caught in the crossfire."

And I don't want Emily caught in the crossfire, he thought. *Which is why I'm leaving her here.* There was really no other choice. He would get Donner, one way or another. The past, and Max, couldn't be forgotten. And he couldn't pretend it had never happened, not without finding some justice.

It would be only too easy to get wrapped up in Emily's problems. *It would be much too easy to get wrapped up in Emily.* But he wouldn't. Judd was afraid Emily could easily make him reevaluate himself and his purpose. Arresting Donner and seeing him prosecuted had to remain a priority. But he was beginning to feel like a juggler in a circus, wanting his time with Emily, and still needing to seek vengeance on Donner.

He'd have all weekend to spend with Emily before anything more could be done on the case. His body tightened in anticipation with just the thought. Somehow he'd have to manage—without letting her get hurt.

He only hoped Emily understood his motivations.

8

"I WANT YOU, Em."

Emily jumped, her heart lodging in her throat. "Good heavens, Judd. You startled me."

His hands slid from her waist to her hips, then pulled her back against him. She could feel the heat of his body on her back, her bottom... "Judd, stop that before John sees."

His growl reverberated along her spine, his mouth nipping on her nape. "John's taking a nap. He's still suffering jet lag."

With shaking hands, Emily carefully laid aside the picture she'd been looking at. She already knew Judd wanted her. He'd made that clear with every look he sent her way. But her brother was here now, and she wasn't comfortable being intimate with John in the house. She cleared her throat and tried to come up with a distraction.

"I don't see anything in these pictures that would prompt anyone to steal them."

Judd pressed closer and his hands came around her waist to rest on her belly. She sucked in a quick breath. His deep voice, so close to her ear, added to her growing excitement. "You have innocent eyes, honey."

"What do you mean?"

"Innocent, sexy eyes." He leaned over to see her face, his gaze dark and searching. "You really don't know what sexy eyes you have, do you?"

It took her a second to remember what she'd been talking about. "No, I... The pictures, Judd?"

His gaze dropped to her mouth and he gave her a soft, warm kiss, then picked up one of the photos. His expression changed as he looked at it, turning dark and threatening. "The guy in the doorway of the deli is an associate of Donner's. My guess is, he only visits this part of town when making a deal. Since the deal surely concerns guns, I'd say he's the one who instigated your break-in."

Emily gave the photo another look. "Really?"

Judd cursed, then tossed the picture back on the kitchen counter. "Unfortunately, I can't do anything about it yet without taking the risk of tipping off Donner and blowing my cover. If we grab this guy, we put a halt to the deal, and lose our advantage." He tightened his mouth. "That's not something I'm willing to do."

"I see." But she didn't, not really. Why was Judd so upset?

"Do you? Do you have any idea how I'd love to get my hands on that guy—*now*—for scaring you like he did?"

His possessive tone made her heart flutter, and she had to force herself to think about the case. "Then you think he was the one who broke in here?"

"Probably not. Like Donner, he has flunkies to do that kind of thing for him. But your taking this picture has obviously annoyed him. Hopefully, it'll help strengthen our case against Donner, too, and we'll be able to make another connection there once we prosecute."

Emily licked her lips and tried for a casual tone. "Do you think the picture alone will be enough to incriminate Donner?"

Judd shrugged. "Possibly. But I don't want to incriminate him. I want to nail the bastard red-handed."

Emily had known that would be his answer, but still... "Judd, maybe it's time to rethink all this. I mean, is it really worth risking your life—"

He laid his finger across her lips before she could finish. "I'm not giving up, Em. I've already gone too far, and I have no intention of letting Donner win. But in the meantime, until he's put away and everything's settled, I don't want you staying here alone."

So. There it was. Emily knew he was up to something the minute he came back in with the developed pictures. She'd been surveying the pictures, not seeing anything out of the ordinary, when Judd started acting amorous.

Acting, Emily? Can't you feel the man's body behind you? He's not acting. No, and as much as that tempted her, she had to remember he only wanted to stay at her house to protect her. It had nothing to do with actually wanting her. Well, maybe it had a little to do with that, but wanting her wasn't his primary motive. She had to remember that.

Smiling slightly, she said over her shoulder, "My brother will be here with me."

He opened his thighs and pulled her bottom closer to him, his hand still firm on her belly, now caressing. "Not good enough. I want to be certain you're safe."

"I...I'll remember to turn on the alarm system." *Lord, Emily. You sound as if you've run five miles.*

Apparently done with talking, Judd dipped his hand lower and his fingers stroked between her thighs, urging her legs apart and moving in a slow, deep rhythm. The material of her dress slid over her as his fingers probed. Heat rushed through her, flushing her face, making her legs tremble, her nipples tighten. She slumped back against him and her head fell to his shoulder. How could she let this happen again when she still felt embarrassed over her wild display the night before? It was as if she had no control of her reactions.

Judd lifted his other hand to her breast, his fingertips finding a taut nipple then gently plucking.

"Judd—"

"Let me." He nuzzled her throat, his warm breath wafting over her skin. "I love how you feel, Em. I love how you come apart for me."

But you don't love me. She almost cried out at the realization that she wanted his love. She wanted it so bad. All the old insecurities returned, the memories of how she'd tried, just as her brother was trying, to gain a

modicum of real emotion, real affection from someone.
They all swamped her and suddenly she couldn't
breathe. She jerked away, hitting her hip on the counter
and hanging her head so Judd couldn't see her face. She
felt breathless and frightened and so damn foolish.

His hand touched her shoulder, then tightened when
she flinched. "Shh. I'm sorry, babe. I didn't mean to
push you."

He turned her to hold her in his arms, no longer seducing, but comforting. And that seemed even worse.
The tears started and she couldn't stop them.

His palm cradled the back of her head, his fingers
kneading her scalp, tangling in her hair. "Tell me
what's wrong, Em. I'll fix it if I can."

Through her tears, she managed a laugh. He was the
most wondrous man. She pulled away to retrieve a tissue, then cleaned up her tear-stained face before turning back to him. He looked so concerned, so caring, she
almost blurted out, *I love you.* But she managed to keep
the words inside. She had no idea how Judd would feel
about such a declaration, but she couldn't imagine him
welcoming it, not now, not while he had to concentrate
on getting Donner.

"I guess I'm just a little overwrought," she said
lamely. She quickly added, "I mean, with my brother
being here, and worrying over him and the break-in."

Judd still looked concerned, but he nodded. "I understand. Would you like to take a nap, too?"

She'd never be able to sleep. "No. I have housework

to do, and the yard needs some work. And I thought I'd put on a roast to cook for dinner."

Looking sheepish, and somewhat anxious, Judd asked, "You mind if I hang around and help?"

He could be so adorable... *Lord, Emily, are you crazy? The man is devastating, not adorable.* "Of course you're welcome to stay. But you don't have to help out. And I'm still not certain that it's a good idea for you to stay overnight."

"I think it's a hell of an idea. And I insist." When she frowned, he added, "It'll only be for a few days. I have to be back at the bar Tuesday. I have the feeling Donner will approach me then. He's getting restless, and he's made it clear he thinks we'll work well together. Since he doesn't like losing, he'll probably make me an offer that no normal stripper could refuse."

It was a small grab for humor, so Emily dutifully smiled. But inside, she felt like crying. The thought of Judd getting more involved with Donner made her skin crawl. They both knew how dangerous he could be.

"Stop frowning, Em. I should be able to set something up with him, find out when and where his next shipment will be, and then I'll bust him. It'll be over with before you know it."

And he'd go out of her life as quickly as he'd entered it. Emily bit her lip. "I'm worried, Judd."

"Don't be. I can take care of myself."

She supposed that was true, since he'd been doing just that since he'd been a child. But for once, she'd like to see him taken care of.

Just that quick, she had a change of heart. Judd might never love her, but he deserved to be loved. And she could easily smother him with affection. She'd enjoy taking care of him, and maybe, just maybe, he'd enjoy it, too.

They spent the day together, and though she tried, Judd didn't let her do any actual work around the house. She couldn't convince him that she enjoyed getting her hands dirty once in a while, and since he seemed so determined to have his way, she allowed it. Judd followed her direction, and she simply enjoyed her time with him.

He was a pleasure to watch, to talk to. He moved with easy grace, his muscles flexing and bunching. It was almost a shame he wasn't a real stripper, for he was certainly suited for the job.

When Judd suddenly stripped off his shirt, Emily thought he might have read her mind. He didn't look at her, though, merely went back to work. She heard herself say, "Are you performing for me, Judd?"

She'd meant only to tease him, but he slowly turned to face her, and his eyes were intent, almost hot as he caught and held her gaze. "I could be convinced to...in a private performance."

Not a single answer came to mind. She sat there, staring stupidly. Judd walked to her, pulled her close then kissed her. It was such a devouring kiss, Emily had to hold on to him. His tongue pushed into her mouth, hot and wet and insistent. Judd slanted his head and continued to kiss her until they were both breathless.

When he pulled away, she stared up at him, dazed. He drew a deep breath and tipped up her chin. "Anytime, Emily. You just let me know."

After that, she refrained from provoking comments. Judd might handle them very well, but she didn't think she'd live through another one. Instead, she asked about Max, Judd's past, and about his work. She wanted to know everything about him.

Emily went out of her way to show Judd, again and again, how important he was to her. At times he looked bemused, and at times wary. But more often than not, he looked frustrated.

She understood that frustration since she felt a measure of her own. But having her brother there did inhibit her a bit. Of course, so did her unaccountable response to Judd. It was scandalous, the way he could make her feel. But she suspected he didn't mind, even if it did embarrass her, so she decided she'd try to see to his frustration—and her own—once John had gone to bed for the evening.

That thought kept her flushed and filled with forbidden anticipation the entire time they worked.

Midafternoon, John joined them, and Emily was amazed to see how John reacted to Judd. It had startled her that morning when John had spoken so openly to Judd. Usually, her brother was stubbornly quiet, refusing to give up his thoughts, brooding in his silence. But with Judd, he seemed almost anxious to talk. And Judd listened.

Emily was so proud of Judd, she could have cried

again. No one had ever reached her brother so easily. In a way, she was jealous, because she'd tried so hard to help John. But she supposed it took a male to understand, and Judd not only listened, he gave glimpses into his own past, allowing John to make a connection of sorts. They found a lot of things in common, though their upbringings had been worlds apart.

Emily decided she was seeing male bonding at its best, and went inside to give them more privacy.

She was starting dinner when they both walked in, looking windblown and handsome. Judd winked at Emily when he caught her eye, and John laughed.

"A man's coming tomorrow to replace my water heater." She more or less blurted that out from sheer nervousness when Judd started her way. He had that glint in his eyes again, and she truly felt embarrassed carrying on in front of her brother.

But Judd only placed a kiss on her cheek, and flicked a finger over the tip of her nose. "Good." Then he turned to John. "Make sure you're here when he comes. I don't think Emily should be alone in this big house with a strange man."

"I'll be here."

Emily might have objected to their protective attitudes, except that she heard a new strength in John's tone, that of confidence and maturity. She gave both men a tender smile. They stared back in obvious confusion.

Backing out of the room, John said, "I think I'll go watch some TV." But he glanced at Judd, then back to

Emily. "Uh...that is, unless you need me to do anything else?"

"No. You can go do whatever you like."

Once he'd left the room, Emily turned a wondering look on Judd. "How did you do that?"

His grin was smug. "Do what?"

"Turn my little brother into a helpful stranger."

He laughed outright. "First of all, you could stop calling him your little brother. He's a head taller than you, Em. Respect his maturity."

"I hadn't realized he possessed any maturity."

"No, I guess you haven't seen that side of him. But I know Max had to work hard at getting me turned around. And the first thing he did was explain that I was old enough to know better. Put that way, I felt too embarrassed to act like a kid. And little by little, Max pointed out ways to distinguish what it takes to be an adult. Your brother's no different. He just needed some new choices."

Emily stood there feeling dumbfounded by his logic. She had enough sense to know it wasn't that simple, to realize what John needed was someone to identify with, someone who cared. That Judd was that man only made her love him more. "Thank you."

Judd stared at her, his gaze traveling from her eyes to her mouth, then slowly moving down her body. He muttered a quiet curse, and started toward her. Emily felt her heart trip. But the phone gave a sudden loud peal, and Judd halted.

Hoping she looked apologetic rather than relieved, Emily asked, "Could you get that, please?"

It rang two more times before Judd turned and picked up the receiver.

She knew right away that asking him to answer the phone had been a mistake. The look on Judd's face as he tried to explain who he was would have been comical if Emily hadn't already suspected who her caller was.

When Judd held a palm over the mouthpiece and turned to her, she braced herself.

"It's your father, and he wants to talk to John. By the way, he also wants to know who I am and what I'm doing here answering your phone." Judd tilted his head. "What do you want me to tell him, babe?"

Lord, Emily. You're in for it now.

"IT'S OVER and done with, Em. You might as well forget it."

Ha! That was easy for Judd to say. Emily had no doubt her parents were headed home right this minute. Of course, it would take them time to get here, but still, she was already dreading that confrontation.

"Come on, Emily. You know John didn't mean to upset you."

"Of course he didn't. It's just that my parents could rattle anyone." But why did John have to tell them Judd was her boyfriend. Lord, if they showed up before everything was settled, she'd either have to admit Judd was a detective, and accept their unending annoyance for involving herself in something they'd expressly forbidden, or she'd have to tell them he was a...a stripper. She could just imagine their reactions to that.

"I wish I'd talked to them, instead of John."

Judd turned his face away from her. "I offered you the phone, honey. But you just gave me a blank look. I didn't think you wanted to talk to them. And even if you had, what could you have told them? That I was a traveling salesman who just picks up other people's phones?"

She shook her head. "No. But I might have thought of something. And John's been so solemn since he talked with Father. I have no idea what they talked about— other than their conversation about me—but I know it couldn't have been pleasant. John's been sullen and sulky ever since, barely eating his dinner and running off to bed early. I wish he'd talk to me about it."

"He's all right, Em. He just needs a little time to himself."

Emily barely heard him. She stood up and started to pace the room, her mind whirling. Then she threw up her hands in frustration. "Oh, this is just awful. What am I going to do?" She didn't really expect Judd to answer, since he'd only been watching her with a strange look on his face. "You can't possibly realize what a trial my father can be. He's so judgmental, so rigid. Once he takes a stand, he never backs down."

Judd put his hand at the small of her back and nudged her toward the stairs. "Come on. It won't do you any good sitting down here and worrying about it. I'd say you probably have a couple of days before your folks get here, and by then, I'll be gone. So you're probably worrying about nothing."

They were halfway up the stairs, when Emily realized what he'd said. She turned to him and gripped his arm. "What are you talking about?"

He wouldn't look at her, but continued up the steps. "I don't want to cause you any problems. So I'll make certain I'm out of the way before they get here. Maybe John can say he misunderstood the situation, or something."

Judd started to go to the room Emily had given him the night before. She rushed up the remaining steps to catch him. "Wait a minute."

Judd lifted one dark eyebrow in question. "What?"

What are you going to do now, Emily? Just blurt out that you want him? He doesn't really seem all that interested anymore. She swallowed and tried to find a way to phrase her request without sounding too outrageous. "I...um."

Judd frowned and walked closer to her. "What is it?"

She glanced toward her brother's room, then took Judd's hand and urged him away from the door. When they were outside her bedroom, she stopped. Judd made a quick glance at the door, and this time both his eyebrows lifted.

Emily drew a calming breath. "I don't want to disturb John. And I don't want you to misunderstand."

Judd waited.

"It's about what I said before. I didn't mean that I wanted you to leave. I was worrying about John, not myself. My parents might not approve of my having you here, but then, they approve of very little when it comes to me. I'm almost immune to their criticism. But John isn't."

"So you're worried about him, not yourself?"

She didn't want to lie to him, that wouldn't be fair. "I can't say I'm looking forward to explaining you. After all, if I tell them the truth, they might interfere, and then your case could be jeopardized."

"What will you tell them?"

Judd had slowly moved closer to her until he stood only a few inches away. Already she was responding to him, and he hadn't even touched her yet. "I don't know. But I don't want you to—"

He laid one finger against her lips. "You've told me all kinds of things you don't want, Emily. Now tell me what you *do* want."

"You."

The way his eyes blazed after she said it reassured her. Her fingers trembled when she reached up to touch his chest. "I want you, Judd. It's a little overwhelming, what you make me feel. I've never felt anything like it before. But last night, you gave a part of yourself to me. Now, I want to do the same for you."

His eyes closed and he drew a deep breath.

Emily took his hand and placed it against her heart. "Do you see what you do to me? It's probably wrong of me to like it so much—" She had to stop to clear her throat as Judd's fingers curled around her breast. The heat in her face told her she was blushing, both with excitement and with her audacity, but she was determined to tell him all of it. "When I was engaged, I thought I knew what excitement was, and it was wonderful because it was forbidden. I felt wild, and just a little bit sinful. But that was nothing compared to how I feel with you."

"How do you feel?"

"Alive. Carnal." She felt the heat in her cheeks intensify with her outrageous admission, but she continued, "Not the least bit refined."

"God, Emily, you're the most refined, the most graceful woman I've ever seen." His tone dropped and his thumb rubbed over her nipple. "You're also remarkably feminine and sexy. Just thinking about how wild you get makes me so hard I hurt."

She licked her lips, then stepped closer still so she could hide her face against his chest. "There are...things, I've wanted to do to you, Judd."

His body seemed to clench, and his voice, when he spoke, was hoarse, "What...things?"

Smiling, Emily whispered, "Don't you think we ought to get out of the hall before we...ah, discuss it?"

She'd barely finished speaking before Judd had opened her bedroom door and ushered her inside. The light was out, but Judd quickly flipped the wall switch. Now that they were out of the dim hall and she had his undivided attention, Emily felt very uncertain about what she had to say. But Judd was staring intently, and waiting, so she forged ahead.

"The last time...well, I know I took you by surprise."

He traced her mouth with a finger. "You can surprise me anytime you like."

"That's not what I mean. You see, even though I try very hard to be proper..." She glanced at his face, saw his fascination, then carefully pulled his teasing fingertip between her lips. Her tongue curled around him as she gently sucked and she heard him gasp. She licked at his flesh, lightly biting him.

"Oh, Emily."

She forgot he watched her with intense scrutiny. She forgot that such displays could be embarrassing. She could only think of the many things she wanted...

She released his finger and he dropped his hand to her buttocks, cuddling her. With a deep breath and a nervous smile, she blurted out, "I'm afraid I'm a fraud. I'm not at all proper. At least, you see, not when I'm..."

"Turned on?" His words were a breathless rasp.

She gave a painful nod of agreement.

There was no smile now, but his eyes showed wicked anticipation, and a touch of something more, something she couldn't recognize. "Are you turned on now, Em?"

The rapid beating of her heart shook her. Heat pulsed beneath her skin, making her warm all over, making her nipples taut, her belly tingle. It was so debilitating, wanting him like this. "Very."

"And you want to do...things? To me?"

Again, she nodded, feeling the husky timbre of his voice deep inside herself. "If you wouldn't mind."

His long fingers curved over her bottom and began a rhythmic caressing. "Tell me what things, Em."

Pressed so close to his body, it was impossible to ignore the length of his erection against her belly, or the warmth of his breath fanning her cheek. She went on tiptoe and nuzzled her mouth against his throat. "I want to taste you...everywhere."

His hands stilled, then clenched tight on her flesh. Against her ear, he whispered, "Oh, yeah."

She pulled his shirt open, and rubbed her cheek over the soft, curling hair there. "I'd like to have you... beneath me, so I could watch your face. You are such an incredibly handsome man, Judd. When you stripped for me...at least, it felt like it was just for me..."

"It was. It made me crazy, the way you ate me up with your eyes. I had to fight damn hard to keep from embarrassing myself that day."

Not quite understanding what he meant, she tilted her head back and stared up at him. "How so?"

His lips twitched into a smile. "You make me hard, Em, without even trying. But watching you watch me... It was the first time I thought stripping was a turn-on. Before that, it was only damn embarrassing."

"I'm looking forward to watching you again."

He groaned, then kissed her, sucking her tongue into his mouth. Emily almost forgot that she wanted to control things this time, but with a soft moan, she pushed Judd away.

"Emily..."

"No, wait." She had to pant for breath, but she was determined. "Will you take your clothes off for me, Judd?"

He blinked. "Will I... How about we take them off together?"

Reaching for his shirt, she said, "Of course," but Judd stopped her hands.

"I meant, we should take *our* clothes off, Em. I want you naked, too. All those things you want to do to me, well, I want to do them to you."

Her mouth went dry. Just the thought of Judd kissing her... She shook her head. "No. Not a good idea. This is my turn..."

"Let's not argue about it, okay?"

She could see the humor in his gaze, and his crooked smile. He was so endearing, so charming, so... "I've never undressed for anyone before."

There. She'd made that admission. She knew her face was scarlet, but she simply hadn't considered that he might want her to display herself. He was the stripper, not her.

Even as his fingers went to the waistband of his jeans, Judd murmured, "Fair's fair, Em." His eyes challenged her, and while her fascinated gaze stayed glued to his busily working fingers, Emily nodded.

She started to untie the bow to her dress, but Judd caught her hands. "No. This one is mine. I thought about doing this—so many times—since we first met." He took the very tip of the lace tie between his finger and thumb, then gently tugged. It pulled open and the ends landed, curling around her breasts. Judd carefully separated the looped strips, while the backs of his fingers brushed over her nipples again and again. Then he slid the tie—so very slowly—out of her collar. Through it all, Emily didn't move.

It was the most erotic thing she'd ever had done to her.

She barely noticed when Judd tucked the lace tie into the back pocket of his jeans. And then he began stripping again, prompting her with a look to do the same. She felt horribly awkward, and very self-conscious. Her body wasn't perfect like his, but rather too slim, too slight. Where Judd looked like every woman's vision of masculine perfection, she was a far sight from the women's bodies displayed in men's magazines.

After unbuttoning her dress, she stepped out of her shoes, trying to concentrate on what Judd was doing, rather than on her own actions. Next, she took off her nylons, tossing them onto the chair by her bed. She saw Judd go still for a moment, then saw his nostrils flare. It hit her that her disrobing excited him. He'd already removed his shirt, and now his jeans, along with his underwear, were shoved down his legs. He stepped out of them, then fully naked, he turned his attention to watching her. There was no disguising his state of arousal. His stomach muscles were pulled tight, and his erection was long and thick and throbbing.

She drew a shuddering breath. "Judd?"

"Go on, honey." When she still hesitated, he said, "You're doing fine, Em. Now, take off the dress."

His words hit her with the impact of a loud drumroll, and she couldn't swallow, her throat was so tight. She saw a slight smile hover on his mouth, and he said,

"I've had some fantasies, too, babe. And seeing you strip is one of them."

"I can't."

"I'm not talking about doing it in front of an audience. It'll just be you and me." Then he lowered his gaze to where her hands knotted in the dress. "Take it off, Em."

She wanted to, she really did. But it wasn't in her to flaunt her body, not when she felt she had nothing to flaunt. She looked away, feeling like a failure, afraid she'd disappointed him. Tears of frustration gathered in her eyes, and just when she would have begun a stammering explanation, Judd touched her.

"Shh. It doesn't matter, honey." He pulled her close again. Emily kept her face averted.

Judd pushed the dress down her shoulders, then worked it lower. The soft material slid over her arms and caught, for just a heartbeat, on her narrow hips, then went smoothly to the floor.

Judd's breath left him in a whoosh as his gaze dropped to her black lace panties and stayed there. Emily suddenly didn't feel quite so awkward, not with the intense, heated way he watched her, as if she were the most fascinating woman he'd ever seen. She skimmed off her bra, then offered him a small, nervous smile.

"Incredible." His gaze finally lifted from her panties to her face. "If I'd known what you were wearing under that dress, I never would have lasted this long." He lowered his head for another long, heated kiss, and at the same time, slid his hands into her underwear, his large warm palms cradling her bottom. His fingers explored, probing and stroking, and Emily clung to him. Before the kiss was over, her panties had joined the rest of their clothes and then she urged Judd to sit on the side of the bed. She dropped gracefully to her knees before him, then reached out and encircled his erection with both hands. He was breathing hard, his thighs tensed, his hands fisted on the bed at his sides. Emily leaned forward, feeling her heart pound, and took a small, tentative lick. He jerked, and a rough broken groan escaped him.

Emily felt encouraged and anxious and excited. She leaned forward again, rubbing her breasts against his thighs, her nipples tingling against his hairy legs. Then she closed her mouth around him, gently suckling and sliding her tongue around him, feeling him shudder and stiffen. Judd gave a long, low, ragged groan and twined his fingers in her hair, leaning over her and holding her head between his large palms, urging her to the rhythm he liked. His hands trembled. So did his thighs.

For the first time in her life, Emily was able to indulge in her sensual nature. Judd encouraged her, praised her, pleaded with her. She loved the scent of his masculinity, the texture of his rigid flesh, so silky smooth and velvety. She gave him everything she could, and he gave her the most remarkable night of her life. She knew, if Judd left her now, she wouldn't regret a single minute she'd spent with him.

And she also knew she'd never love another man the way she loved Judd Sanders.

9

THE BAR WAS CROWDED as women waited for the show to begin. Emily felt a twinge of jealousy, thinking of all those women seeing Judd in his skimpy briefs, but she kept reminding herself it was necessary for him to perform.

She'd left John, still acting contrary and withdrawn, at her house. It seemed it only took one phone call from her father to destroy all the headway Judd had made with her brother. Judd told her not to worry, that he was certain John would work everything out. But John was her little brother, and she couldn't help worrying about him any more than she could stop worrying over Judd.

He was obsessed with catching Donner. Anytime Emily tried to discuss it with him, he went every bit as silent and sullen as John. She supposed he had to get into a certain mind-set to be able to work his cover. After all, not many men could pull off being a stripper. But she hated seeing him act so distant. Even now, as he lounged beside her sucking on an ice cube he'd fished from her cola, she wanted to touch him, to somehow reach him. But he ignored her.

"There aren't any men here tonight. It doesn't seem likely that Donner will come."

She knew Judd had heard her, despite her lowered voice. But he didn't look at her when he replied, "He'll come. I feel it. And there aren't any men because it isn't allowed. It's ladies' night. But Donner has free run of the place. He'll be here."

The look in his eyes, the way he held himself, was so different from the Judd she knew. She felt alone and almost sick to her stomach. She had wanted Donner so badly, but now, she only wanted to protect Judd. From himself. From his feelings. And most especially from his self-designed obligations to a dead man.

Before Emily could comment further, Judd glanced at the watch on his wrist, then said, "I have to go get ready."

He straightened, and Emily tried to think of something to say, anything, that would break his strange mood. Then Judd leaned down and lifted her chin with the edge of his fist. "Do me a favor, babe. Don't watch. If you do, I'll start thinking about last night, and I might not make it."

Emily blinked. "I thought you wanted everyone to believe we had an…intimate association."

"Oh, they'll believe." Then he kissed her. Emily heard the bartender hoot, and she heard a few of the women close by whistle. One particularly brazen woman offered to be next.

Judd practically lifted her from the bar stool, one hand anchored in her hair, the other wrapped around her waist. The kiss was long and thorough, and couldn't have left any doubts about their supposed relationship.

Pulling back by slow degrees, Judd said, "Damn, but I want to be home with you. Alone. Naked."

Emily hastily covered his mouth. "Hush. You'll have me so rattled, I won't remember what I'm doing here."

He kissed her fingers, then straightened again. "Stay out of trouble. And stay where I can see you."

"But don't watch?"

"You've got it." Then he flicked a finger over her cheek and walked away to his "dressing room." Emily couldn't hold back a smile. *He wasn't as indifferent as you thought, was he, Emily? Who knows, this may all work out yet. Maybe, if enough time passes without Donner showing, Judd will finally give up and let someone more objective handle the case.*

Emily was daydreaming about having a future with Judd, when Clayton Donner strolled in the front door, along with his bully boys. Emily sank back on her stool to avoid being noticed. Not that she was all that noticeable, with so many women in the room.

Donner stopped inside the door and spoke with one of his men. He checked his watch, smoothed a hand over his hair, then opened a door leading to a set of stairs. Mick, one of the men from the pool hall, stayed at the bottom. Minutes later, another man entered and spoke quietly with Mick. Emily sucked in a sharp breath as she realized he was the man from the photograph. Fear hit her first, knowing this man had deliberately sent someone to break into her home. But anger quickly followed.

Whoever he was, he could be no better than Donner. And Emily wanted to see them both put away—preferably without involving Judd.

Their heads were bent together in a conspiratorial way, and Emily wished she could hear what they were saying. When Mick led the other man upstairs, she decided she would follow. She felt a certain foreboding, not for herself, but for Judd. She had to protect him.

Her heart pounded with her decision.

Judd was probably the most capable man she'd ever met, but his love for Max would make him vulnerable in ways that could endanger his life. If there was some way, any way, to help predict Donner's actions, she could use the information to help Judd.

With that thought in mind, she waited until Judd had been cued by his music and walked onto the dance floor, then she slipped away. Judd didn't notice since he seemed to be making every effort not to look her way. Women screamed in the background and the music blared. But above it all, Emily heard the rush of blood in her ears and her thundering heart. She tried to look inconspicuous as she made her way to the door.

It opened easily when she turned the knob, and she held her breath, waiting to see if anyone would be standing on the other side. She could always claim to be looking for the ladies' room. But once the door was open, she was faced with a narrow flight of stairs, with another door at the top.

Oh, Lord, Emily, don't lose your nerve now. And stop breathing so hard or they'll hear you. Each step seemed to echo as her weight caused the stairs to squeak. As she neared the top, she could make out faint voices and she strained to listen. Donner's tone was the most prominent, and not easy to miss. He had a distinctive sound of authority that grated on her ears.

Trying to draw a deep, calming breath, Emily leaned against the wall and concentrated on picking up the discussion, hoping she'd hear if anyone moved to open the door. Gradually, she calmed enough to hear complete sentences, and minutes later, she started back down the stairs.

Her hands shook horribly and she thought she might throw up. When she opened the door and stepped back into the loud atmosphere of the bar, her vision clouded over and she had to shake her head to clear it.

Nothing had ever scared her like eavesdropping on Clayton Donner. But she now had what she needed to protect Judd. She knew when, and where, the next shipment would be bought. A plan was forming, and she'd have a little more than a week to perfect it. She'd make it work, and best of all, it wouldn't include Judd.

JUDD FINISHED UP his act just as Emily slid back onto her stool. She was stark white and her face seemed pinched in fear. He felt an immediate surge of anger. Something had upset her, and he wanted to know what.

Ignoring grasping hands as he left the floor, he strode to Emily and stopped in front of her. She met his gaze

with wide brown eyes and a forced smile. A crush of
women began to close in behind him and he took Emily's arm without a word, then started toward the room
where he changed. As he walked, he glanced around,
hoping to catch sight of Donner or one of his men. He
saw only grinning women.

When he closed the door behind them, she began to
chatter. "The crowd seemed especially enthusiastic tonight. It's a shame you're not really a performer. You're
obviously very good at it."

Judd didn't offer a comment on that inane remark.
He studied her face, saw her fear and wondered what
had happened. "Where did you go, Em?"

"Where did I go?"

"That's what I asked." He tossed his props aside and
picked up a towel to rub over his body. Emily watched
his hands, as she always did, with feminine fascination.
"You were gone the entire time I danced."

"Oh." She pulled her gaze up to peer into his face,
then shrugged. "I went to the ladies' room."

"Uh-uh. Try again."

She tried to look appalled. "You don't believe me?"

"Not a bit." Maybe she had seen Donner. Maybe the
bastard had even spoken to her. Judd felt his shoulders
tense. "Where did you go, Em?"

She gave a long sigh, then looked down at her feet.
"All right, if you must know, I was jealous."

That set him back. "Come again?"

She waved her hand airily. "All those women were

ogling you as if they had the right. I couldn't bear to watch. I suppose I'm just a...a possessive woman."

Judd narrowed his eyes, mulling over what she'd said. She sounded convincing enough, but somehow, her explanation didn't ring true.

Emily gave him a defiant glare when he continued to study her. "How would you feel if the situation were reversed? What if that was me dancing, and other men...were ogling me?"

She blushed fire-red as she made that outrageous suggestion, and Judd felt a smile tug at his mouth, despite his belief she was keeping something from him. He pulled on his jeans and then said to her, "I suppose I'd have to take you home and tie you to the bed. I sure as hell wouldn't sit around while other men enjoyed the sight of you. I'm a little possessive, too."

"There! You see what I... You are?"

Shrugging into his shirt, Judd said, "Yes, I am. And because I'm so possessive, I'd like to know what you're up to."

She immediately tucked in her chin and frowned. Judd was just about ready to shake her, when a knock sounded on the door. He went still, his adrenaline beginning to flow, then he moved Emily out of the way and opened the door.

Mick stood there, an insolent look on his face.

"Yeah?" Judd forced himself not to show any interest.

Mick frowned. "Clay wants to talk to you."

"Tell Clay I'm busy." As he said it, he reached back

and wrapped an arm around Emily. She seemed startled that he'd done so.

Mick's gaze slid over Emily, then came back to Judd. "He said to tell you he'd like to discuss a little venture with you."

"Ah. I suppose I can spare a few minutes, then. Where is he?"

"Upstairs. I'll take you there."

"I can take myself. Tell him I'll be there when I finish dressing." He shut the door in Mick's face.

Emily immediately started wringing her hands. "Don't go."

"What? Of course I'm going." He leaned down and jerked on his socks and shoes. His hands shook, the anticipation making simple tasks more difficult. He looked up at Emily. "This is what we've been waiting for. Don't go panicking on me now."

As he was trying to button his shirt, Emily threw herself against him. "It's too dangerous. You could get hurt."

"Em, honey." He didn't want to waste any time, but he couldn't walk out with her so upset. He drew a deep breath to try to collect himself. "Em, listen to me." When he lifted her chin, she reluctantly met his gaze with her own. "It'll be all right. Nothing's going to happen here in the bar. I'm only going to talk to him. I promise."

Her bottom lip quivered and she sank her teeth into it to stop the nervous reaction. Judd bent to kiss her, helping her to forget her worry. "I want you to wait at the bar for me. Stay by Freddie until I come back out. Promise me."

"I'll stay by Freddie."

"Good." He opened the door and urged her out. "Now, go. I won't be long."

Judd leaned out the doorway and watched until Emily had taken a stool in the center of the long Formica bar. He signaled Freddie, waited for his wave, then went back into the room, stuffed his props into his leather bag and hoisted it over his shoulder. He took the steps upstairs two at a time. He rapped sharply on the door. His jaw felt tight and there was a pounding in his temples.

Mick opened it, peeked out, then pulled it wide for him to enter.

Donner stood and came to greet him. "Well, if it isn't our friend, the stripper. Tell me, do the ladies ever follow you home?"

Judd forced his muscles to relax. "They try sometimes. But my calendar is full."

"Ah, yes. I almost forgot. The little bird from the pool hall."

Judd didn't reply. He wanted to smash his fist against Donner's smug, grinning face. Instead, he forced a negligent smile.

"Do you enjoy dancing...Sanders, isn't it?"

"That's right. And no, not particularly." Then he pulled a wad of money from his pocket, all of it bills that had been stuffed into his briefs. "But it pays well."

"I can see that it does. There are easier ways to make money, though."

Judd settled back against the wall and folded his arms across his chest. He was so anxious, his mouth was dry. But he kept his pose, and his tone, almost bored. He gave a slow, relaxed smile, then said, "Why don't you tell me about it."

JUDD WAS still trying to figure out how he was going to keep Emily out of the picture. He couldn't risk her by taking her along, but if she was told the truth, she'd insist on coming with him. They'd argue, and she'd end up with hurt feelings.

He couldn't bear the thought of that. Her feelings were fragile, and she was such a gentle woman, the thought of upsetting her made him feel like an ogre. But dammit all, he had to keep her safe. *Max was dead, but Emily was very much alive.* He had to make certain she would be okay.

Eight days. Not long enough, but then, no amount of time would be enough with Emily. The way he felt about her scared him silly, and it had been a long time since he'd felt fear. Growing up in the wrong part of town, with his father so drunk and angry and unpredictable, he'd gotten used to thinking fast and moving faster. Which was maybe why he'd never settled down with any one woman.

He wouldn't settle down now, either.

He couldn't. Not with Emily. She deserved so much more than he could ever give her, more than he'd ever imagined possessing. Not material things—she had those already, and he wasn't exactly a pauper. He could provide for her. But emotional things? Family and background and happy memories? He couldn't give her that. But he wanted to. So damn much.

She reached over and touched his shoulder as he drove through the dark, quiet streets of Springfield. "What happened, Judd? You've been so quiet since talking with Donner."

He couldn't tell her the truth, so he lied. And hated himself for it. "Nothing happened. He questioned me a little. Tried to feel me out. But he didn't give me a single concrete thing to go on."

"So..." She swallowed, looking wary and relieved. "So you don't know yet what his plans are?"

"No." He flicked her a look. The streetlights flashing by sent a steady rhythm of golden color over her features. She was so beautiful. "I guess we'll have to keep up the cover a little longer. I, ah, suppose I can let you out of it if you think it'll pose a problem. I mean, with John being home now and all."

"No!" She gripped his arm, then suddenly relaxed. "No. I don't mind continuing...as we have been."

A little of his tension eased. He desperately needed a few more days with her. Once it was over, he'd have no further hold on her, and he wouldn't be able to put off doing the right thing. But for now... He tugged on her hand. "Come here, babe."

Emily slid over on the seat until their thighs touched and her seat belt pinched her side. She laid her head on his shoulder. Judd felt a lump of emotion that nearly choked him, and he swallowed hard. For so long, he'd been driven to get Donner and to avenge Max's death. He'd thought doing so would give him peace and allow him to get on with his life. But he realized now, after claiming Emily as his own for such a short time, there would be no peace. His life would be just as empty after Donner was convicted as it had been before. Maybe even more so, because now, he knew what he was missing.

EMILY FELT like a thief. She was getting rather good at sneaking around. It still made her uneasy, but with Judd always watching her so closely, the subterfuge was necessary.

In order to "protect" her, he'd sort of moved in. It was a temporary situation, prompted by Judd's concern over the break-in. He'd never once made mention of any emotional involvement, but his concern for her was obvious. And though it made her plans that much more difficult to follow, she was glad to have him in her home.

During the day he teased her and talked with her; he made her feel special. And at night...the nights were endless and hot and carnal. Judd touched her in ways she'd never imagined, but now craved. The shocking suggestions he whispered in her ear, the things he did to her, and the greedy, anxious way she accepted it all, could only be described as wicked—deliciously wicked. She loved his touch, his scent, the taste of him. She loved him, more with every day.

They had to be discreet, with John in the house, slipping into bed together after he was asleep, and making certain to be up before him. But John seemed to take great pleasure in having Judd around, even trying to emulate him in several ways. The two men had become very close.

Emily had thought long and hard about her situation with Judd, and her main priority was to take every moment she could with him. She suspected John might be aware of their intimate relationship, but since she would never ask either man to leave, there was no help for it. And she simply couldn't feel any shame in loving Judd.

Now, as she slipped from the bedroom an hour before the sun was up, Emily thought of her plan. She knew Donner would be making his deal tomorrow at the abandoned produce warehouse on Fourth Street. She had her camera loaded and ready. If she could get a really good, incriminating picture, there would be no reason for Judd to continue his investigation. He would be safe.

Giving Judd the evidence he needed would be her gift to him, to help him put the past to rest. Then maybe he'd want her to be a part of his future.

She was at the kitchen table studying a map when she heard Judd start down the steps. Seconds later, when he entered the kitchen, she tried not to look guilty. The map, now a wadded, smashed ball of paper, was stuffed safely in a cabinet drawer.

"What are you doing up so early, babe?"

Emily drank in the sight of him, standing there with his hair on end and his eyes blurry. There was so little time left. After tomorrow, his case would be over, the threat would be gone and Judd would leave her. She rushed across the floor in her bare feet and hugged him.

Judd seemed startled for a moment, and then his arms came around her, squeezing tight. "What's wrong, Em?"

"Nothing. I just couldn't sleep."

He set her away from him. "Take a seat and I'll start some coffee."

She sat, and fiddled with the edge of a napkin. "Judd?"

"Hmm?"

"I have some stuff I have to do tomorrow. Around two."

His hand, searching for a coffee mug, stopped in mid-reach. When he turned around, he wore a cautious expression and his posture seemed too stiff. "Oh? What kind of stuff?"

"Nothing really important. I have a load of clothes to drop off at the shelter, and some packages to send to an aunt for her birthday." She held his gaze, striving for a look of innocence. "And I think I'll do a little grocery shopping, too."

All at once he seemed to relax and his breath escaped in a sigh, as if he'd been holding it. He gifted her with a small smile. "Well, don't worry about me. I'm sure I can find something to occupy my time. In fact, I should go check on my mail and maybe pay a few bills."

Emily congratulated herself on her performance. She'd been brilliant and he'd believed every word. Now, if she could only get him to leave before her so she wouldn't have to try to sneak out. He'd surely notice her clothes, dark slacks and a sweater, since he'd never seen her wear anything like them before. She liked the outfit. It made her feel like 007.

An hour later, all three of them were finishing breakfast. It was a relaxing atmosphere, casual and close, like that of a real family. Emily smiled, thinking how perfect it seemed.

That's when her parents arrived.

THE INTRODUCTIONS were strained and painful. Judd remembered now why he'd never done this. Meeting a mother, especially when you were barefoot and hadn't shaven yet could make the occasion doubly awkward. He thought about bowing out, letting Emily and John have time alone with their parents, but one look at their faces and he knew he wasn't going to budge.

"What is he doing here, Emily?"

"I told you, Mother, he's a friend."

"What kind of friend?"

"What kind do you think, Father?"

Judd winced. He'd never seen Emily act so cool, or so defensive. And her smart reply had Jonathan Sr. turning his way. "I think you should remove yourself."

Judd raised an eyebrow. Well, that was blunt. Before he could come up with a suitable reply, Emily fairly burst beside him.

"You overstep yourself. This is my house, and Judd is my guest."

That startled Judd, but evidently not as much as it did Emily's family. They all stared, and Emily glared back. "Uh, Em..."

"No." She raised one slim, imperious hand. "I want you to stay, Judd."

Evelyn Cooper stepped forth. She was an attractive woman, with hair as dark as Emily's and eyes just as big. For the briefest moment, Judd wondered if this was what Emily would look like when she got older—and he felt bereft that he'd never know.

"We have family business to discuss, Emily. It isn't proper for a stranger to be here."

John snorted. "He isn't a stranger, he's a very good friend. And he already knows all about me. I trust him."

Evelyn narrowed her eyes at her son. "I wasn't talking about your irresponsible behavior. You will, of course, return with us. We've found the perfect surgeon." Then her gaze traveled again to Judd. "I was speaking of Emily's...unseemly conduct."

Judd was still reeling over the way John had just defended him. He was a friend? A very good, trusted friend? He felt like smiling, even though he knew now wasn't the time. Then Evelyn's words sank in. *Unseemly?*

John had told him that Emily never stood up to her parents, that she took their insults and their politely veiled slurs without retaliating. Probably because she still felt guilty for misjudging her fiancé and causing her parents an embarrassment. But to put up with this? He didn't like it, but he also didn't think he should interfere between Emily and her parents. He drew a deep breath, and tried to remain silent.

Emily lifted her chin. "I'm not entirely certain John wants to see another surgeon, or that it's at all necessary."

"John will do as he's told."

"Despite what he wants?"

Jonathan Sr. harrumphed. "He's too young to know what he wants, and certainly too irrational at this point to make a sound decision. It's possible the scars can be completely removed. Appearances being what they are, I think we should explore every avenue."

Judd stood silently while a debate ensued. John made it clear he didn't want any further surgery. The last doctor had been very precise. The scars would diminish with time, and beyond that, nothing more could be done. Judd thought it was a sensible decision on the boy's part, but John's father disagreed. And though he'd told himself he wouldn't interfere, Judd couldn't stop himself from interrupting.

"Will you love your son any less with the scars?"

Both parents went rigid. Then Jonathan shook his head. "This has nothing to do with love!"

"Well, maybe that's the problem."

That brought a long moment of silence. Evelyn looked at her husband, and then at her son. "We only want what's best for you."

"Then leave me alone. I'm sick of being picked over by a bunch of doctors. I did a dumb thing, and now I have some scars. It's not great, but it's not the end of the world, either. They're just scars. I'd like to forget about what happened and get on with my life."

Jonathan frowned. "What life? Skulking around in the slums and getting into more trouble? We won't tolerate any more nonsense."

"Is that why you wanted to keep me out of the country? Dad, I could find trouble anywhere if that's what I really wanted. But I don't." He looked at Judd, then sighed. "I'm sorry for the way I've acted. Really. But I want to stay here now. With Emmie."

Jonathan shared another look with his wife, then narrowed his eyes at Emily. "I'm not certain that's a good idea. Emily's always been a bad influence on you."

Judd waited, but still, Emily offered no defense. It frustrated him, the way she allowed her parents to verbally abuse her. Again, he spoke up, but he kept his tone gentle. "It seems to me Emily's been a great influence. Didn't you just hear your son apologize and promise to stay out of trouble? What more could you ask for?"

Evelyn squeezed her eyes shut as if in pain. "Good Lord, Emily. He's just like the other one, isn't he? How much will it cost us this time to get you out of this mess?"

Judd froze. They couldn't possibly mean what he thought they meant. He looked at Emily, saw her broken expression and lost any claim to calm. But Emily forestalled his show of outrage.

"How dare you?"

She'd said it so softly, he almost hadn't heard her. The way her parents stared, they must have doubted their ears, too.

"How dare you even think to compare them?" Her voice rose, gaining strength. She trembled in her anger. "You don't know him, you have no idea what kind of man he is."

Judd was appalled when he saw the tears in her eyes. He touched her arm. "Emily, honey, don't." She hadn't defended herself, but she was defending him? He couldn't bear to be the cause of dissension between her and her family. It seemed to him they had enough to get straight without his intrusion.

Emily acted as though he weren't there. She drew herself up into a militant stance and said, "I would like you both to leave."

Jonathan glared. "You're throwing us out?"

"Absolutely. I've listened long enough to your accusations and disapproval. I won't ever be the daughter you want, so I'm done trying."

Evelyn laid a hand to her chest. "But we just got here. We came all the way from Europe."

Emily blinked, then gave a short nod. "You may have ten minutes to refresh yourselves. Then I want you gone." And she turned and walked out of the room.

Judd started to go after her when he heard Jonathan say, "You're not good enough for her, you know."

He never slowed his pace. "Yeah, I know."

But before he'd completely left the room, he heard John whisper, his tone filled with disgust, "You're both wrong. They're perfect...for each other."

WHAT DID KIDS KNOW? Judd asked himself that question again and again. So John liked him. That didn't mean he could step in and do something outrageous like ask Emily to marry him. No, he couldn't do that.

But he could let her know how special she was, how perfect...to him.

When he found her in the bedroom, she was no longer crying. She sat still and silent in a chair, her back to the door, staring out a window.

"You okay?"

"I'm fine."

She wasn't and he knew that. He made a quick decision, then knelt beside her chair. After smoothing back her hair, he brushed his thumb over her soft temple. "Maybe you should go talk to them, babe. No yelling, no silent acceptance. Talk. Tell them how you feel, how they *make* you feel. They love you, you know. They don't mean to hurt you."

She didn't look at him. "How do you know they love me?"

Because I love you, and I can't imagine anyone not loving you. "You're a beautiful, giving, caring person. What's not to love?"

Her face tilted toward him, and he saw a fresh rush of tears. He kissed one away from her cheek. "Talk to them, Em. Don't let them leave like this." He stroked her cold fingers, then enfolded them in his own. "Anything can happen, I learned that with Max. Time is too short to waste, and there are too many needy people in the world to turn away those that love you."

She squeezed her eyes shut and tightened her lips, as if trying to silence herself. Judd stood, then pulled her to her feet. "Go. Talk to them. I'll get showered and dressed."

"In other words, you intend to stay out of the way?"

He grinned at her grumbling tone. "I think that might be best. But I'll be here if you need me."

She stared up at him, her eyes huge, her lashes wet with tears, and Judd couldn't stop himself from kissing her. He'd wanted to spend this last day with her, to fill himself with her because after tomorrow, he'd have no reason to be in her house, no reason to keep her close. No reason to love her. He pulled back slowly, but placed another kiss on the corner of her mouth, her chin, the tip of her nose.

"You'd better get a move on before they leave. The ten minutes you gave them is almost up."

She laughed. "If you knew my parents, you'd know how little that mattered. They think I'm on the road to ruin. I doubt they're about to budge one inch." Then she hugged him. "Thank you, Judd. You're the very best."

As she left the bedroom, he grinned, hoping she'd work things out, and wondering at the same time...the best of what?

10

UNFORTUNATELY, it rained. Emily felt the dampness seep through her thick sweater and slacks. But she supposed the rain was good for one thing—it made her less conspicuous lurking around the back of abandoned warehouses.

Leaving today hadn't been too difficult. Judd had gone on his errands before her, and her parents, though they had stayed in town, hadn't remained at her house. They had talked a long time yesterday, and her mother had said they hoped to "work things out." They'd been apologetic, and they'd listened. Emily wondered at their change of heart, and if they'd still feel the same after she went against their wishes and brought charges against Clayton Donner.

This particular produce warehouse had several gates where a semi could have backed up to unload its goods. Three feet high and disgustingly dirty, the bottom of the gate proved to be a bit of a challenge as Emily tried to hoist herself up. The metal door was raised just enough for her to slip through, and although she still had time before Donner was due to arrive, she wanted to be inside, safely ensconced in her hiding place so there'd be no chance of her being detected.

The flesh of her palms stung as they scraped across the rough concrete ledge. Her feet peddled air before finding something solid, and then she slid forward, wedging herself under the heavy, rusting door. She blinked several times to adjust her vision, then wrinkled her nose at the stale, fetid air. Donner had certainly picked an excellent place to do his business. It didn't appear as though anyone had been inside in ages.

Emily got to her feet, then hastily looked around for a place where she could hide, and still be able to take her pictures. The warehouse was wide-open, so she should be able to capture the deal on film. The entire perimeter was framed with stacks of broken crates and rusted metal shelving, garbage and old machine parts. Not a glimpse of the vague light penetrating the dirty windows reached the corners, so that's where Emily headed. She shuddered with both fear and distaste. But she reminded herself that it could easily have been Judd here, risking his life. That thought proved to be all the incentive she needed.

Just as she neared the corner, she heard the screeching whine of unused pulleys and one of the gates started to move. With her heart in her throat, she ducked behind the crates and crouched as low as she could. She wondered, a little hysterically, if they would hear her heart thundering. She listened as footfalls sounded on the concrete floor, and voices raised and lowered in casual conversation. Then she forced herself to relax; no one was aware of her presence.

When Donner and the man from the picture came to

stand directly in front of her, not twenty feet away, Emily silently fumbled for her camera. A van backed up to the gate, and the driver got out—Emily recognized him as Mick—and began unloading wooden cases. She almost smiled in anticipation, despite her nervousness.

Just a few more minutes and... A soft squeaking sounded near her. Emily didn't dare move, her heart once again starting on its wild dance. Then she heard it again. She very carefully tilted her head to the side and peered around her. Then she saw the red eyes. *Oh my Lord, Emily!* A dark, long-bodied rat stared at her.

She drew a slow deep breath and tried to ignore the creature. But it seemed persistent, inching closer behind her where she couldn't see it. She felt the touch of something, and tried not to jerk. The camera was in her hands, she had a clear shot between the crates where she hid, and Donner was winding up his business. All she needed was a single picture.

The rat tried to climb the crate beside her, using her leg as a ladder. Emily bit her lip to keep from breathing too hard. And she was good, very good. She didn't make a single sound.

But the damn rat did.

A broken crate collapsed when the rodent tried to jump toward her, and in a domino effect, other containers followed and Emily found herself exposed. She fell back, trying to hide, but not in time. Within a single heartbeat, she heard the click of a gun, then Donner's voice as he murmured in a silky tone, "Well, well. If it isn't the little bird. This should prove to be interesting."

JUDD CURSED, not quite believing what he'd just seen. How had she known? He'd been so damn careful, even going as far as faking frustration to make her believe that the deal had been called off. But somehow she had found out. And now she was inside, with Donner holding a gun on her. He lowered himself away from the window, then swiped at the mixture of rain and nervous sweat on his forehead. His stomach cramped.

Cold terror swelled through him, worse than anything he'd ever known, but he pushed it aside. He couldn't panic now, not if he hoped to get her out of there alive. His men were stationed around the warehouse, but at a necessary distance so they wouldn't be detected. Judd had planned to make the deal, recording it all through the wire he wore, then walk out just as his men arrived, making a clean bust. Now he'd have to improvise.

Speaking in a whisper so that Donner and the others wouldn't hear, he said into the wire, "Plans have changed. We'll have to move now, but cautiously. There's a woman inside, and I'll personally deal with anyone who endangers her." He allowed himself one calming breath, then said, "I'm going in."

With icy trickles of rain snaking down his neck, he took one final peek through the grimy window, then lowered himself and inched forward until it appeared he'd just arrived directly at the back entrance of the warehouse. His stance changed to one of nonchalance, and he walked through the door beside the gate.

Emily looked up at him in horror. Mick, his grin feral,

held her tightly, with her arms pulled behind her back. Donner and the other man stood beside him. Judd feigned surprise, then annoyance. "What the hell is she doing here?"

Donner smiled, then inclined his head. "I'd thought to ask you that when you arrived. You're late."

With a casual flip of his wrist, Judd checked his watch. "Four o'clock exactly. I'm never late. Now, what's she doing here? I didn't want her involved."

"As you can see, she's very much involved." Donner held up a camera. "I believe she had some photography in mind."

"Damn." Then he stomped over to Emily. "I thought I told you to knock that crap off?"

He gave an apologetic grimace to Donner. "She's been thinking of doing a damn exposé on the east end. She's taken pictures of every ragtag kid, every gutter drunk or gang punk she can find. Annoys the hell out of me with that garbage."

Donner gave a lazy blink. "I think she's stepped a little over the line this time."

Judd lifted an eyebrow. "Got some interesting pictures, did she?" He turned to Emily, chiding her. "You just don't know when to quit, do you?"

"Actually," Donner persisted, "I don't think she took a single photo. But that's not the point, now, is it?"

Judd crossed his arms over his chest. "If you mean what I think you mean, forget it. I'm not done with her."

"Oh?"

"She promised to buy me a Porsche. I've been want-ing one of those a long time."

Donner moved his gaze to Emily. With a nod from him, Mick pulled her arms a little tighter. The dark sweater stretched over her breasts and her back arched. Judd had to lock his jaw.

"After today, you won't need her. We can make plenty of money together." He dropped the small cam-era and ground it beneath his heel, then paced away from Emily. "Get it over with. We've been here too long already and there's plenty more to do." As he spoke, he watched Judd.

Knowing Donner was waiting for a reaction, Judd did his very best to maintain an air of disgust. But his mind raced and he tried to gauge his chances of taking on all three of them. He planned his move, his body tense, his mind clear.

The man from the picture grinned. He hefted an au-tomatic weapon in his hand, the very same make that had been sold to Emily's brother. He held the gun high in his outstretched hand and aimed at Emily. Judd roared, lurching toward him, just as the gun exploded.

EMILY SQUEEZED her eyes shut, so many regrets going through her mind, all in a single second. She'd been a fool, a naive fool, thinking she could help, thinking she might make a difference. She'd ruined everything, and now Judd would die, because of her.

She heard the blast of the gun and jerked. But she felt no pain. A loud scream tore through the warehouse, echoing off the stark walls. She opened her eyes and realized the man who'd intended to shoot her was now crouching on the cold floor, his blackened face held in his hands. Blood oozed from between his fingers. The gun had backfired?

Judd reacted with enraged energy. His fist landed against Donner, who seemed shocked by what had just happened. She felt Mick loosen his hold and she threw herself forward, landing hard on her knees and palms, her shoulders jarring from the impact.

And then the room was flooded with men.

There was so much activity, it took Emily a moment to realize it was all over, that Donner and his men were being arrested. Judd appeared at her side, helping her to sit up.

"Are you all right?"

His voice sounded strange, very distant and cold. She brushed off her palms, trying to convince her heart that everything was now as it should be. Her throat ached and speaking proved difficult. "I'm fine. Just a little shaken."

Lifting her hands, Judd stared at her skinned palms, and his eyes narrowed. "I think you should go to the hospital to get checked over."

After flexing her shoulders, still sore from the way Mick had held her and the impact on the hard floor, Emily rubbed her knees. "No. That's not necessary—"

"Dammit! For once, will you just do as I tell you?"

Her heart finally slowed, in fact it almost stopped. He sounded so angry. She supposed he had the right. After all, she'd really messed things up and nearly gotten them both killed. *You might as well begin apologizing now, Emily. From the looks of him, it's going to take a lot to gain his forgiveness.* She reached out to take his hand. "Judd, I—"

He came to his feet in a rush and his eyes went over her, lingering on the dark slacks. He ground his jaw and looked away. An ambulance sounded in the distance, and when Emily looked around, she realized the man who'd been about to shoot her was very seriously wounded. Donner looked as though he wasn't feeling too well, either. He'd been close enough to receive some of the blast from the gun, and he bore a few bruises and bloody gashes from his struggle with Judd.

A passing officer caught Judd's eye, and he was suddenly hauled over to stand before Emily. Judd seemed filled with annoyance. "See that she gets to the hospital. I want her checked over."

"Yes, sir."

Remarkably, Judd started to walk away. Emily grabbed for him. Her hands shook and her heart ached. "Judd? Will I see you later at the house?"

He didn't look at her. "I already got my stuff out. Your house is your own again. Go home and rest, Em. We can question you later."

She watched him walk away, not quite believing her eyes, not wanting to believe it could end so easily. And then it didn't matter anymore. She wasn't giving up. She may have been a fool, but she refused to remain one. She wanted Judd, and she'd do whatever it took to get him.

HE CUT HER COLD. Emily tried numerous times to reach Judd. Three weeks had passed, and the police no longer needed her as a witness. Evidently, Judd no longer needed her...for anything.

She had no reason to seek him out, but she still tried. He'd remained at the small apartment. She'd been there several times, but he either didn't answer the door, or he was so distantly polite, asking her about her brother, wishing her well, that she couldn't bear it. They might have been mere acquaintances, except that Emily felt so much more. She loved him, and even though her parents tried to convince her not to make a fool of herself, she couldn't give up.

She had tried apologizing to him for mucking things up. That had made him angry all over again, so she'd refrained from mentioning it further. John had gone to him once, to see how he was doing. Judd received her brother much better than he'd received her, and Emily felt a touch of jealousy. It bothered her even more when John claimed Judd was "absolutely miserable."

"He wants you, Emmie. I know he does. He just doesn't realize you want him, too."

Much as she wanted to believe that, she couldn't allow herself false hope. "I've made it more than clear, John. I can't very well force the man to love me."

But John had shrugged, a wicked grin on his face.

"Why not? At least then you'd settle things, one way or another."

She thought about that. How could she "force" a man who was nearly a foot taller and outweighed her by ninety pounds? She decided to try talking to him one more time, and went directly to his apartment. His old battered truck sat out front, and as Emily passed, something different caught her eye. At first, she had no idea what it was, and then it struck her.

She bent next to the driver's window and peered inside. The black lace that used to hang so garishly from his rearview mirror had been replaced by the tie from her dress. Emily vaguely remembered that night when Judd had shoved the pale strip of material into his back pocket moments before they'd made love.

And now it had a place of prominence in his truck.

It was ridiculous how flattered she felt by such a silly thing, but she suddenly knew, deep in her heart, that he did care. At least a little.

She remembered the day he'd allowed her to indulge her fantasies. He'd said he had fantasies of his own, and he'd whispered erotic suggestions to her while they made love, wicked things about her really stripping—performing for him. She had been mortified and excited at the same time. Some of the things he'd suggested had been sinfully arousing, and she'd promised herself, once she could gain the courage, she'd fulfill every single one of his fantasies.

But she hadn't. She'd let inhibitions get in her way, even though she knew how wild it would make him.

But maybe it wasn't too late. Maybe she could still set things right between them, and show him how much she loved him by giving him everything she possibly could.

She started away from the truck, her confidence restored. But she stopped dead when a little old lady blocked her path.

"What were you doing there, girl?"

"I..." What should she say? That she was admiring an article of her clothing, strung from a rearview mirror like a masculine trophy? That she intended to seduce a man? *Get a grip, Emily.* "I was just about to call on my...brother. I see his truck is here, so I know he must be—"

"He ain't home. He's taken to walkin' in the park every evening. Usually picks up a few necessaries for me while he's out."

"I see." Emily's disappointment was obvious.

"I'm the landlady here. You want me to give him a message?"

"No. I had hoped to...surprise him." Her mind whirled. "It's his birthday today. And since he doesn't have any other family, I thought maybe I could make this day...special."

"His birthday, you say? Well, now we can't let it go by without a little fun, can we? I could let you into the apartment, if that's what you're wantin'."

Already Emily's pulse began racing. "Yes, that would be wonderful. And I promise, he'll be so surprised."

JUDD DRAGGED himself up the steps to his apartment. The weather had been considerably mild lately, and he wore only a T-shirt with his jeans. The early-evening air should have refreshed him, but he still felt hollow. He'd felt that way ever since Emily had been endangered—by his own design.

His drive, his need to see Clayton Donner sent to jail, had clouded his reason and cost him his heart. He'd thought losing Max had been the ultimate hurt, but knowing he'd endangered Emily, knowing he'd risked her life, used her, loved her, was slowly killing him. He couldn't bear to face himself in the mirror.

He also knew he'd love her forever, and it scared the hell out of him. Time and distance hadn't helped to diminish what he felt. But what could he do? Ask her to forgive him, to spend her life with him? How could he? She deserved better than him. Her grace was always with her, whether she was working at the soup kitchen, or sneaking into a warehouse full of danger. She was elegance personified, and he was a man who went to any extreme to get what he wanted, to see a job done, including stripping off his clothes for a pack of hungry women.

Self-disgust washed over him. He rubbed his face, wishing he could undo the past and be what Emily deserved.

Mrs. Cleary met him in the hallway, a huge smile spread over her timeworn features. Struck dumb for a moment, Judd stared.

"Did you fetch my bread and eggs?"

"Here you go, Mrs. Cleary. Are you sure you don't need anything else?" Judd had taken to the older woman with her gruff complaints and constant gossip. He figured she was probably every bit as lonely as he was.

"No, I got all I need. Now you run on home. And happy birthday."

Judd blinked. "But..." She winked at him, and he decided against correcting her assumption. Age could be the very devil, and if she wanted to believe it was his birthday, for whatever reason, he'd let her. "Thanks."

When he reached his apartment and stepped inside, he knew right away that something was different. He could feel it. All his instincts kicked in, and he looked around with a slow, encompassing gaze. His bedroom door was shut.

That seemed odd. Then odder still, music began to play. He recognized the slow, brassy rhythm as one of his favorite CDs, and his instincts took over. Without real thought, he inched his way to the cabinet where he kept his Beretta, slowly slid it into his palm, and crept forward.

The beat of the music swelled and moaned, and Judd flattened himself beside the door. Then, with his left hand, he slowly turned the knob and threw it open.

He waited, but no bodies came hurdling out, and he cautiously, quickly, dipped his head inside then jerked back to flatten himself against the wall.

No. It took his mind a second to assimilate what he'd

just seen, and still, he didn't believe it. He blinked several times, then peeked into the room again.

Yes. That was Emily.

Standing in the center of his rumpled bed.

He moved to block the doorway, his gun now held limply at his side. The black leather jacket he'd used as part of his stripping costume hung around her shoulders, the sleeves dropping past her fingertips. It wasn't zipped, and he could see a narrow strip of bare, pale flesh, from her black lace bra to her skimpy lace panties. Her navel was a slight shadow framed by the zipper and black leather.

Max's hat sat at a rakish angle on her head. She grinned.

Sweat on his palms made it necessary for him to set the gun aside. He stumbled to the dresser, then took two steps toward her before he stopped, unsure of himself, unsure of her.

With her eyes closed, her hips swayed to the music. As he watched, her face blossomed with color—and the jacket fell away.

He licked his lips, trying to find some moisture in his suddenly dry mouth. It had been three long weeks, three *endless* weeks, since he'd made love to Emily. She lifted her arms over her head, her nipples almost escaping the sheer lace, and he felt his body harden. His erection grew long and full, pressing against his suddenly tight jeans.

She turned on the bed, not saying a single thing. Judd breathed through his mouth as his body pulsed, his eyes glued to the sight of her small bottom encased in black lace. Her hips swayed and his erection leaped, along with his heart.

Emily reached behind her back to unhook her bra. He took another step closer. He wanted to ask her what this meant, but he was afraid to speak, afraid she'd stop—afraid she wouldn't. When she turned around, she tossed the bra to him.

It hit him in the chest and fell to the floor. He couldn't move. He couldn't blink. He could barely force air past his restricted lungs.

The hat fell off when she bent slightly at the waist, hooking her thumbs in the waistband of her panties. The blush had spread to encompass her throat, her breasts. Her pointed nipples flushed a dark rose. The music picked up, hitting a crescendo and crashing into a final, raging beat.

Emily released the panties and they slid down her slender thighs, landing against his disheveled covers and pooling around her feet.

Judd stared at the triangle of dark glossy curls and his nostrils flared. He started toward her.

She raised one hand and he stopped. "We need to talk, Judd."

"Talk?" His mind felt like mush, his body, like fire.

"I realized desperate measures were necessary to get your attention."

"Believe me, Em. You have my attention." It was an effort, but he managed to force his gaze to her earnest face.

She lifted her chin. Her lips trembled for a moment. "I hope you'll understand. Sometimes we have to do outrageous things to meet our ends. Just as you had to strip to trap Donner, well, I had to strip to…trap you." She clenched her hands together, and then she blurted out, "I love you."

"You…" He'd been engrossed with her odd comparison, and the fact she'd evidently understood his motives all along. And she hadn't blamed him for doing whatever needed to be done. He'd been wrong about that.

But now his thoughts crashed down. She couldn't have said what he thought she'd said. "You…love me?"

"Yes. I love you. I want you. Forever. I realize I'm not quite what you had in mind for a…a woman."

"A wife?"

"Well, yes. That would probably be the most logical thing, considering how I feel."

"You love me?"

She made an exasperated sound and propped her fists on her naked hips. His body throbbed.

"Didn't I just say so? Twice?"

"I believe you did."

"Well? Do you think you can come to love me? I realize this is probably not very…fair of me. To try to seduce you—"

"You passed 'try' when the music began."

"Oh. I see. Well, then, you should know, I expect everything. Our...reactions to each other are...very satisfying, but I want more."

"You want me to marry you?"

She tromped over to the edge of the bed, bringing her breasts a mere foot from his face. He swallowed, then gave up trying to keep his gaze focused.

He put first one knee, then the other on the bed and wrapped his arms around her, pressing his mouth to her soft naked belly. "I love you, too, Em. God, I love you."

Her fingers clenched in his hair. "Really?"

"I was afraid to love you, but it happened, anyway."

"You were afraid?"

He nodded, then nuzzled one pointed nipple. "You deserve so much better."

Her fingers tightened and pulled. Wincing, he looked up at her. "Don't you ever say that again! You're the finest, the most caring man I've ever known."

He saw her intent expression, her anger, and felt himself begin to believe. "Our backgrounds—"

"Damn our backgrounds!"

Judd blinked. Cursing from Emily? He felt shocked, and ridiculously happy.

"You rose above your upbringing, Judd. Despite all your disadvantages, you're a hero." Her fingers tightened again and she brought his head against her. "You're my hero."

"No."

"Yes! I'm not giving you pity, because you don't need it. I'm only giving you the truth. I love everything about you." She swallowed hard, then gentled her hold on his hair, smoothing her hand over his crown. "And you make me feel loved. Nothing else matters. We can work out the rest."

"The rest?"

"I love my house, Judd. I'd like us to live there."

"I'd...I'd like that too. But Emily, I'm not a pauper. I've never had anything to spend my money on, so I have a hefty savings—"

Her fingers touched his mouth. "I never thought you were helpless, Judd. And we'll support each other, okay? That is, if you can tolerate my parents. They do seem to be trying."

He pulled her down until she knelt in front of him. "Marry me, Emily."

Her eyes, those huge, eat-a-man-alive eyes, fairly glowed with happiness. She kissed him, all over his face, his ear, his shoulder. "Yes," she shouted, "Oh, Judd, I love you."

As they both began trying to wrestle his clothes from his body, Judd said, "Promise me you'll strip for me again later. You took me so much by surprise, I think I might have missed something."

Her blush warmed him, and she smiled. "Whatever you say, Detective." And then he made love to her.

HARLEQUIN®

Temptation

and

HARLEQUIN®

I N T R I G U E ®

Double Dare ya!

Identical twin authors Patricia Ryan and
Pamela Burford bring you a dynamic duo of
books that just happen to feature identical twins.

Meet Emma, the shy one, and her diva double,
Zara. Be prepared for twice the pleasure and
twice the excitement as they give two
unsuspecting men trouble times two!

In April, the scorching **Harlequin Temptation** novel
#631 **Twice the Spice** by Patricia Ryan

In May, the suspenseful **Harlequin Intrigue** novel
#420 **Twice Burned** by Pamela Burford

Pick up both—if you dare....

HARLEQUIN®

LOVE *or* MONEY?
Why not Love *and* Money!
After all, millionaires
need love, too!

How to Marry a MILLIONAIRE

Suzanne Forster,
Muriel Jensen
and
Judith Arnold

bring you three original stories
about finding that one-in-a million man!

Harlequin also brings you
a million-dollar sweepstakes—enter
for your chance to win a fortune!

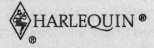

HARLEQUIN ®
®

Look us up on-line at: http://www.romance.net

HTMM

#635 THE BLACK SHEEP
by Carolyn Andrews

Meet Nick Heagerty. Loner. Rebel *with* a cause.
Ten years ago, he was driven from his home, unjustly
accused of a crime he didn't commit. And he's never
looked back. When a family emergency crops up, he
had no choice but to return—but not for long. Then
he meets gorgeous Andie Field. And suddenly,
Nick realizes his wandering days are numbered.

All men are not created equal. Some are rough
around the edges. Tough-minded but tenderhearted.
Incredibly sexy. The tempting fulfillment of every
woman's fantasy.

When it's time to fight for what they believe in, to
win that special woman, our Rebels and Rogues are
heroes at heart.

**Look for THE BLACK SHEEP in May 1997,
wherever Harlequin books are sold.**